MURDER WITH MEANS

BLYTHE BAKER

Sylvia is still struggling with the terrible secret she has learned about Miles, when she is dealt a fresh blow. During a visit to an art museum, she unknowingly becomes the last person to speak with a murder victim alive.

Forced to set aside her misgivings, Sylvia must trust Miles enough to lean on his help once again. Together, can the pair catch an elusive killer before the trail goes cold?

1

"You know, Sylvia, a little bit of sleep would do wonders for those dark circles under your eyes."

I blinked, my eyes dry and itchy. Swinging my head around, I fixed my gaze on my younger sister Joan seated at the piano near the window. Her fingers danced over the keys in no particular order or sequence, rather playing with the sound and testing the notes together.

I didn't quite have an answer to her statement, as my mind ticked along in a fog, evident by the chess set before me. Pieces had not been moved for more than five minutes, and I couldn't seem to formulate any sort of idea as to where I might move next. It was as if the answers were smoke that I simply couldn't grab hold of, and they would vanish before I had the chance to dwell upon them.

She spoke the truth, though not in a terribly kind manner. I wanted to chide her for being too frank...but how was that any different than the way she always was?

"She's right, you know," said my mother, who was seated across from me. She seemed far more interested in the hat she held in her hands, which she was pinning strings of pearls and dried roses onto, than she was in our game. She gave me a pointed look, her eyes the same shade of cobalt blue as Joan's. "Would it really be too much for us to ask that you *not* stay up all hours of the night reading? You haven't changed that habit since you were a child, have you?"

Still I didn't quite know how to respond. I pinched my eyes shut a brief movement before opening my mouth with the hopes of words trailing out. "That... that isn't why I haven't been sleeping."

An unpleasant and harsh jolt of piano keys made me jump. I looked over at Joan just as she swung herself around on the piano bench and rose to her feet.

"Don't tell me..." Mother said, a fresh coat of coyness in her tone. "Is this about a new romance?"

I didn't seem to have the strength to be irritated with her. "No..." I said. "It has nothing to do with anything like that."

A movement near the fireplace drew my attention.

Miles, our new butler, was bending down to lay cut logs into the grate of the fireplace. Flames licked the sides of the shorn wood.

"Then what could possibly be troubling you so much that you aren't sleeping?" my mother asked, a note of exasperation in her voice. "The only reason why *I* could never sleep was because of your father." She giggled. "Oh, how his letters used to keep me up, dreaming of him and pining for him..."

As pleased as I was with my mother's affection for my father, it concerned me little when she likely would have no difficulty ignoring what had really been bothering me.

Joan slumped down into the chair beside me, her eyes narrowed slightly as they often were when her mind was working to solve a problem. "It's about Mr. Morrow, isn't it?"

Even Miles turned to look at the sound of that man's name. It had not been uttered again since the day Miles had brought me home from confronting him.

I turned to gaze at Joan. How was it that she could see through me so clearly, so easily? Was it written across my face?

"Father told me not to speak of him any longer..." I said in a low tone. It might not have been so hoarse, had I not deliberately been so silent over the past two weeks.

"He certainly did," Mother said. "And quite frankly, *I* do not wish to hear anything about him anymore, either. You had best listen to your father."

Joan continued to stare at me, her gaze piercing through my exhaustion, her arms crossed and jaw working as if she had not heard me in the first place. "It makes sense, really," she said. "Given the whole ordeal, it's only natural that it would be keeping you awake."

Miles lingered near the fireplace, his back still to me. He reached up to rearrange a few mementos on the mantle, only to move them back again. I tried to ignore him, even as he was so clearly not ignoring me or the conversation he was undoubtedly overhearing.

I didn't wish to discuss this with an audience, especially not with Mother. She would have preferred me to sit there and gossip with her over the latest superficial matters in her circle of friends, rather than to listen to the genuine struggles I had. In truth, perhaps she had little idea of what to do or say to help me, and so she would rather simply avoid the subject all together.

"Oh, come now..." Mother said. "It's all over and done with. Everyone is all right, yes? You are fine, Sylvia. You are safe at home, with all of us. That's what matters. We can all just...move on, and be happy, can't we? Of course we can." The grin she wore was growing tiresome, for no matter how much she wore it, it seemed to be entirely lacking any sort of genuine feeling. She didn't believe it, and we certainly did not, yet she still tried her best to keep up the façade of no trouble or strife in our household, despite the evidence to the contrary.

"Are you having trouble falling asleep? Or are the memories plaguing your dreams?" Joan asked.

"Joan, dear, I don't think – " Mother began.

"Hold on, Mother. If she tells us, then we can better help her," Joan said, holding up her palm in Mother's direction. "What is it, Sylvia?"

I hesitated with every ear waiting to hear what thoughts I would formulate, but I could not bring myself to voice any of them. "It's – "

I glanced toward Miles, for the briefest of moments. *This is not all about Mr. Morrow...*I mused, unable to lie to myself. *This is just as much about Miles as it is about the rest of it.*

Joan seemed determined to stare the answer out of me, perhaps believing she could frighten the truth forth, with enough pressure. She might have in the past, but with Miles standing so close...and with my guilt at knowing I had been the reason we might very well have brought on a potential murderer as our butler...

I looked down at the chessboard, the pieces still waiting to be moved. The game could continue to wait, for all I cared about it now.

What I had found in Miles' room, in his personal

belongings when I had helped him move to the other side of the house... I had not been able to forget it. No matter how much I had tried to forget that small newspaper clipping, or what the article had said...the picture of the young woman standing with a man who was so obviously Miles...knowing that she was dead, and that he had been the one police suspected as her killer...

It made sense that he was good at moving around unseen, that he had shown in the past that he knew exactly what to look for in connecting others to crimes. No wonder he had been such a help to me recently, when I was trying to find out who had murdered my uncle. I had succeeded in tying Mr. Morrow to the crime, largely because of Miles' assistance. And now I had to question where he had learned those skills, and how he might next put them to use. Had he truly killed his late wife, back in London?

"I suppose I have just had so much on my mind that..." I struggled to string the words together in a coherent way. I wanted to maintain some semblance of privacy about this matter, at least until I had a chance to learn more about it. I wasn't yet ready to confront Miles with what I had learned.

"That what, darling?" Mother asked, a surprising edge to her words. She had produced an ornate paper fan and begun to flutter it before herself. How could she possibly be warm, when the temperatures had been steadily dropping for the past three days? "Honestly, you *must* finish your thoughts. It is a very irritating habit to leave a statement unfinished."

"I suppose I just haven't put it all behind me yet," I said finally, choosing to speak to Joan. "Every time I try and close my eyes to rest, my mind fills with the images of that night, and of Uncle Walter, and..." *And that newspaper article and photo I found tucked away in the book in Miles' room.*

"As I said, it makes sense," Joan said with a nod. "It is not at all unusual for someone to have nightmares or trouble sleeping after traumatic events. The best thing you can do is to distract yourself. Your mind needs a rest and a chance to think of something happy and good. That will help remind you that you aren't trapped there in that moment and that life has continued on."

I stared at her. "I do seem to be reliving it too often," I said. Even as the words left me, the moment that Mr. Morrow toppled over the banister, falling to his death, played once again in my thoughts.

Joan nodded. "Indeed," she said. "I imagine it to be a great deal like running a race. Eventually, you grow so tired you simply *must* walk in order to finish it, yes? You won't get over it if you never give yourself a chance to heal."

*Give myself a chance to heal...*I pondered.

Miles shifted from the fireplace, coming around

the back of the couch and stationing himself at the table where he had brought our afternoon coffee. Diligently, he filled another cup and brought it over to my mother.

"Oh, thank you Miles," she said with a sunny smile. "You really are wonderful, always knowing what I need."

"You are quite welcome, madam," Miles said politely.

I watched him turn away, and frowned. Every time I saw him treat my family and I with such care, it made less sense to me. I had trusted Miles right from our first meeting, so much so that I had brought him into this house to work for us. The new knowledge that he was not who he seemed to be was hard to come to grips with.

You also thought well of our old friend Mr. Morrow, though, didn't you? I asked myself.

I hated the thought but it continued to surface. Every memory I had of Frank Morrow had been tainted. It was as if I had lost a happy part of my childhood, as if it had been stolen away from me.

"We all have such moments," Joan said. "Moments wherein we simply cannot believe what has happened. What is important is to realize they are a part of life, that they come along with the beautiful times as well."

I studied her, momentarily grateful for her encouragement, before my memories caught up with me. "I might have been impressed with such wisdom...if I didn't remember those words are from the closing monologue of a character you played at last summer's festival."

Joan didn't appear sheepish, as I thought she might. "And?" she retorted. "Does that make it any less true?"

"No," I admitted. "I suppose it doesn't."

She shook her head. "You have been through a great deal, but consider trying to put it behind you now. Remember that life can be happy and exciting."

"I suppose you are right," I said.

I thought of my father, who after learning the truth about Mr. Morrow had been quite reclusive. Of course, he was also still distracted by money matters and the recent crash on Wall Street. Our personal finances had not turned out to be as badly impacted as expected, because Father's real estate investments had retained more value than his stocks. Still, there remained some lingering tension. Between that and the death of my uncle, followed by the betrayal of Mr. Morrow, Father had much to brood about.

Perhaps I am more like Father than I realize, but I don't want to make the same mistakes. I must move on.

"And it seems, if I am not mistaken..." Joan began, hopping to her feet and striding over to the writing desk along the wall. "...That you received an invitation a few days ago. From Catherine Waters, wasn't it?"

I had forgotten all about it. "I did, yes," I said.

"Were you planning to go?" Joan asked.

I blinked. Had I even opened it?

"I don't know..." I said lamely.

Miles glanced at me from his post near the table; I hadn't noticed that he was scraping fresh cinnamon sticks into a bowl. I wondered if they would be for some sort of dessert later.

"I believe that came yesterday, Miss," he told me. "If I am not mistaken, it is an invitation to one of the art exhibits in town."

How in the world does he know that? I wondered.

"Indeed it is," Joan said, turning it end over end, examining the back of the card. "Down near Central Park, in fact. That will be pleasant, this time of year."

"What does it say?" I asked, holding my hand out.

She passed the invitation to me.

The invitation itself was a flyer to said exhibit, titled *Sea of Glass*, the edges painted with strokes of pale blue and green watercolor. It gave the date and times, November 9th at 7:00 pm. "That's this Saturday," I said, eyebrows rising. "Two days from now."

Joan shrugged. "You still have time to accept," she said. "When was the last time you saw Catherine? Because I cannot remember."

"I don't know either," I said.

"Oh, what a pleasant young woman Catherine is," Mother said, piping up again now that the conversation had taken a turn more suited to her tastes. "Always so unpredictable and energetic. I do like her."

I turned the note attached to the invitation over in my hand. "She says I am welcome to bring you too, Joan," I said. "If you are interested in coming." I hoped she would see plainly on my face that I wanted her to attend with me.

Joan nodded. "I think I am available that day," she said. "It should be fun! A great way for you to get your mind off...well, all of it, really."

Mother clapped her hands together. "How wonderful!" she exclaimed. "Perhaps Catherine could come here for gossip and hors d'oeuvres before you all go."

"Yes, Mother," Joan said. "I am certain that could be arranged."

Mother looked over her shoulder at Miles. "Miles, be a dear and run to the kitchen to tell Gibbins we are having a guest on Saturday afternoon."

"Certainly, madam," Miles said with an inclination of his head. Just before leaving, he turned his green eyes on me and locked me with his gaze.

I hadn't spoken to him alone in nearly two weeks. A question remained in his eyes, as it did every time he looked at me. He obviously wondered why I had not allowed myself the chance to be alone with him, to speak of all that had happened to us both during our investigation into my uncle's death. It had been in the aftermath of that adventure that I had found the article about Miles, the information that had changed everything. I knew he would somehow find out what I had seen among his things. It was only a matter of time until he found a way to draw it out of me...and then what?

For now, I needed to wrestle with myself and put it all behind me, so that I could stand being in the same room as him.

Mother and Joan descended into conversation about what we should wear to the exhibit and what might be acceptable late autumn refreshments, but all I could think about was Miles, as he departed from the room.

Eventually, I would need to speak with him. I knew as much. I would need to discover the truth and not have his secret hanging over us both forever. I thought of the look on his face when he had once hinted to me that he had been hurt or wronged in some way in the past, that he had gained experience from it, yet did not wish to discuss the details. Was he possibly referring to that article? Was that why he had come all the way here to New York? Had he fled England?

I wondered, not for the first time, if I wasn't simply misconstruing what I had read in the newspaper article. It was such a small piece with hardly any information in it. Or perhaps, if I was honest, I just didn't want to believe that Miles was in any way like Mr. Morrow, that he could willingly take the life of another person...

let alone a wife he had never spoken of. Her very existence had been a revelation to me. Anyway, it wouldn't be the first time a journalist had made a sweeping claim that ended up being incorrect. And who knew just how the newspapers in England were, whether they were fair or not?

Miles could have been wrongly accused of the crime, either by the press or the police, simply for being at the wrong place at the wrong time. But did I trust him enough to assume him innocent, when those with more knowledge of the situation evidently thought otherwise? Could I allow myself to behave as if that were the truth?

I didn't know. Not yet.

I had trusted him implicitly before I had learned all of this, but there was no turning back now, was there? I couldn't simply forget what I had seen. Especially if, by bringing such a person into our home, I had brought myself and my own family into danger. If he had killed someone once, who could say he would not do it again someday?

And yet...he didn't seem like a man capable of murder. I had seen what taking a life had done to Mr. Morrow. It had unhinged him. I imagined it took part of his soul, a part he would never be able to recover or repair. Once the truth had been uncovered, the horror and guilt plagued Mr. Morrow, morphing him into a hollow shell of what he once had been.

Miles didn't look or behave like that.

Unless he is incredibly good at hiding his true self, unless he is an unfeeling monster who carries no guilt or regret...

"Well?" Joan asked, looking at me impatiently. "What do you say about the art exhibit? We *are* going, aren't we?"

I didn't need to spend any more time inside my own head. Surely a night out would be exactly what I needed?

"All right," I said. "Let's go to the exhibit."

Mother chortled, clapping her hands. "Lovely! It's about time we had some *good* excitement in this house!"

I smiled weakly and tried to believe that was the only kind of excitement that lay ahead of me from now on.

2

"The *Sea of Glass* exhibit, I have heard, was inspired by Mr. Vincent's trip down the coast," said Catherine, a friend I had made some years ago when I had spent a summer in Albany. She had been visiting her aunt and uncle while I had been staying with my grandparents, and we had become almost inseparable. Time and responsibilities had drawn us away from one another, but being in her presence once again reminded me why I had been so fond of her in the first place.

Her smile spread across her face as she gestured to a long, ivory wall adorned with nothing but canvases filled with color.

"And *of course* you know the great Mr. Vincent Garden, yes?" she asked.

"The artist," Joan said, unblinkingly. "Renowned in

New York, and growing in popularity in London, Paris, and Rome. That Mr. Vincent Garden?"

"Right you are," Catherine said with a snap of her fingers, beaming. "He is an incredible painter with unrivaled skill."

"And all these pieces..." I asked, looking around at the square room we had wandered into, the lights overhead bright and warm. "He painted them?"

The landscape closest to me boasted brilliant blues and pale greens, colors that seemed so incredible they could have only been seen at the height of summer... and only found in nature. Puffy clouds filled the cerulean sky, kissing the perfectly straight line of the horizon. It seemed as if I stared at the real sea through a window. It was breathtaking.

Just beside that painting hung another, much longer and narrower piece of a sunset in golds, oranges, and pinks. There was periwinkle in the highest parts of the sky and the inky blue water was streaked with the sunlight. Once again, I might as well have been staring out an open door. I could almost smell the saltiness of the sandy shores.

"He most certainly did paint them, each and every one in this room," Catherine said. "There is a wonderful pamphlet near the front door filled with information about all of the paintings, his inspiration and the places he visited to capture these images."

"The sea is one of the most depicted landscapes in

art, yet each painting is as different as the artists that paint them," Joan said. "I take it the rest of the exhibit is similar?"

"Yes, but not all are done by the same artist or in the same medium," Catherine said. "I shall show you around, of course! You are here as my guests!"

She spun on the spot, grinning at the both of us.

"Now...tell me, how exactly are you connected to all this?" I asked.

"My father is on the board," Catherine said, pointing over her shoulder in the direction of the front doors. I thought I had recognized him when we arrived, though he had greyed a great deal since I had seen him last. "Knowing how much I appreciate art, how many of my friends take part in this community, he knew I would be all too happy to come and see what was happening here this evening. And, as we were so close to your part of town, I thought it only made sense to invite the both of you!"

"Well, we appreciate the invitation, of course," I said. "To be perfectly honest, it was a welcome distraction from the difficulties we have been facing."

The crowd in the room thickened as the top of the hour approached. We might have been at the far end of the gallery, near the blackened windows that surely overlooked Central Park in the light of day, but given the way Catherine spoke of the artist, it only made sense that so many people would be hurrying to catch a glimpse of the displays. Women in their most glamorous dresses, men in pressed suits and ribbon-wrapped hats; all gasped in awe at the paintings around us.

Catherine stared about with immense gratification, tossing her thick, auburn curls over her shoulder. "This is the sort of gathering we all have needed," she said. "The insanity of the world around us beckons, yet we need not heed its call."

"True," Joan said. "But it's difficult to ignore when it seems to have encroached on our very homes."

I gave her a sidelong look, which she returned almost imperceptibly.

Catherine gave a swift wave, as if swatting at a buzzing fly. "This will all pass," she said. "Likely before Christmas, if my father's assumptions are correct. Everything simply needed to slow down, everyone needed to take a step back. It will smooth out, I'm sure of it."

She may have only been talking about economic matters but we had more troubling matters on our minds, and I even more than Joan.

"However..." Catherine said, her brows lifting as she looked over at me. Her grin spread. "There *is* another reason why I hoped you would join me here this evening."

"We might have guessed," Joan said, folding her arms.

Might we? I wondered. I had thought nothing of it, but that could have been due to the fact that I was occupied with other matters.

"I heard your relationship with a certain young Mr. Lawson ended on a rather...sour note," Catherine said. "Nothing you did, of course. The man clearly didn't know what he had with you, thus making the mistake he did."

"Yes, well..." I said, trying to maintain my grip on my smile. "It's all water under the bridge now. We have been amiable the few times we have seen one another."

Joan huffed beside me, rolling her eyes. She thought me too forgiving.

"Yes, but that is why I asked you to come here tonight," Catherine said. She gave Joan an apologetic smile. "I'm sorry that I have no such surprise for you, Joan, but given that you are the youngest anyway, you have plenty of time..."

Joan's brow furrowed and she looked at me out of the corner of her eye.

My somewhat tired mind caught up with the underlying part of the conversation. "Oh, Catherine, you don't mean – "

At once, her arm snaked beneath my own, pinning me to her side like a dog with a tendency to bolt. "You have not even given me the chance to *tell* you about him yet," she said with a whine in her voice that I hadn't heard since we were much younger. "He is *wonderful,* Sylvie, and I promise you will like him. You *will!*" She started to lead me through the dense crowd, as if we were fish trying to swim against the current.

"Was that a promise? Or a threat?" Joan asked, following as close as my own shadow.

"Who is it?" I asked, nervousness already bubbling up inside me. "I don't know if this is the best time for – "

"Nonsense," she said. "You cannot wait on this matter. He will be snapped up before long. Handsome, successful – "

"You still haven't told me who he is," I said.

"That's because you don't know him," she said, attempting to drag me through an open doorway into the next room of the gallery.

I dug in my heels, halting her progress. "Catherine, please," I said.

She turned around to look at me, then pursed her lips together and sagged like a slouching throw pillow. "Very well," she said. She pulled me off to the side, out of the way of traffic. "I didn't tell you because you wouldn't have recognized his name, anyway. At least, you most likely will not have known him."

"That's an odd assumption, given how many friends our father has in the city," Joan said.

"Yes, but I haven't known your father to be deeply

invested in the arts," she said. "But as *you* are, Joan, you might recognize him."

"Is it that Ralph Young?" Joan asked.

Catherine shook her head. "No. He was engaged a few weeks ago."

"What about one of the Henricksons?" Joan asked. "They are around our age."

Catherine's eyes twinkled, but she still shook her head. "No, neither of them. Are you familiar with Mr. Fredrick Adams?" she asked.

Joan's eyes widened, her lips parting in surprise. "Truly?" she asked.

Catherine's smile grew, and she nodded.

I looked back and forth between them. "Wait just one moment," I said. "I have no idea who that is – "

"He isn't already seeing anyone?" Joan asked.

Catherine shook her head again. "No one."

"And did you tell him you were bringing Sylvia here to meet him?" Joan asked.

"I most certainly did," Catherine said, squeezing my arm. "And he was *delighted* at the idea."

I blinked at her, both somewhat flattered and flustered. "What did you tell him, exactly?" I asked.

"Just that you were the daughter of one of the city's most important and affluent men," she said, her smile brimming with pride. "He knew right away when I mentioned your family name. He said he had no idea that Mr. Shipman had grown daughters."

Joan regarded me with curiosity, but all I wished to do was refuse this meeting. *It only makes sense he would want to meet Joan and I. It really has nothing to do with me and everything to do with my father's money. He knows nothing else about me.*

"What do you think?" Catherine asked. "If you absolutely refuse, I will understand...though I will most certainly not be happy with you, given the lengths I went to ensure he could be here tonight."

I sighed. "I don't want to embarrass you after you've gone to such trouble..." I thought of saying I didn't know how well this interaction would go. Then again, I had come to the exhibit as a means of distracting myself from my life back at home, and this would most certainly be a distraction.

"Who knows, Sylvia," Joan said teasingly. "Maybe this Mr. Adams will turn out to be the man of your dreams."

I smiled doubtfully. "Maybe he will."

"That's the spirit!" Catherine said, standing on the tips of her toes and clapping excitedly. "Shall we go in and meet him, then?"

She pulled me through the doorway she had been trying to drag me through before, into a room that seemed fitting for the *Glass* part of the exhibit. Orbs, crystal clear like bubbles, hung from the ceiling interspersed with lights. Shining pieces of blown glass hung all around the room, or sat atop pillars and pedestals.

Bowls in dark cobalt blues, vases of opaque white, intricately blown sculptures of blue, sandy yellow, and green.

"Over here," Catherine said, once again pulling me along, with Joan following after us.

I hadn't had time to prepare for this. I hadn't done my hair as I might have if I'd known I would be meeting a young man, nor would I have worn this simple dress.

"Mr. Adams?" Catherine asked, reaching a group of people gathered near one of the corners, beside a high narrow window so dark it might as well have been a mirror.

A tall and broad-shouldered man turned at the sound of Catherine's voice, smiling down at her. "Ah, Catherine," he said. "I hoped you hadn't forgotten about me this evening."

"How could I possibly have done that?" Catherine asked with a grin.

His eyes, a silvery blue as cool as mist, shifted to me. They drew me in, stark against his dark lashes. "And might this be Miss Shipman? And perhaps her sister, given how much they look alike?"

Some of the other members of the group turned their gazes to us, hearing our surname mentioned. That surprised me little, given how easily recognized our family was. I could hardly go anywhere without someone knowing my father or having heard of him.

"Yes, indeed," Catherine said. "This is Miss Sylvia Shipman, and her sister Joan."

Mr. Adams turned fully around to us. He held a glass flute in his hand, filled with a bubbling beverage. A smile appeared on his face, making his sharp cheekbones even more pronounced, as he reached up and removed his hat, revealing a head of thick chestnut hair. "I am pleased to meet you both," he said.

"Likewise," Joan said politely, giving me a sharp jab in the ribs with her elbow.

I resisted the urge to massage the spot, instead forcing a smile. "The pleasure is ours, truly," I said, falling back on what I always said upon meeting someone new.

"I was surprised to realize we hadn't had the chance to meet," he said. His voice, though clear and pleasant, was a bit higher than I might have expected, given his height and breadth. "I imagine we have many of the same acquaintances."

"I assume you are correct," I said. "Our father must know half the city, and is aware of the rest."

His small smile grew ever so slightly. "You are quite funny."

Then his gaze moved past me, to Joan. "And am I correct in thinking you are the same Joan Shipman who has performed on the stage in recent years?" he asked.

Joan stiffened beside me. "Yes," she said. "I have on a few occasions."

"Admirable," he said. "Acting is a difficult, unforgiving art form. There are many who perhaps hold too high a standard for those gifted with the courage to grace a stage like that."

"Mr. Adams would certainly know about talent," Catherine said with an arched brow. "He is an art critic, after all."

A critic? I mused. That certainly seemed interesting that Catherine had fallen in with this sort of group.

"Oh, but that isn't to say I have anything negative to say of your performances, of course," Mr. Adams said. "From what I have heard, you have a great deal of talent."

"Thank you," Joan said.

I glanced at her, seeing a glow about her that I hadn't expected.

"How do you and Catherine know one another?" I asked him.

"We met this summer at a charity gala," Mr. Adams said smoothly. "Catherine's father was kind enough to invite along some of us who frequent the gallery."

"It was more of an exhibit, really," she said. "Much like this one."

"That one paled in comparison to this," Mr. Adams said. "Those amateur paintings could hardly be considered art."

"Yes, well, there were hardly any recognizable artists there that evening," Catherine said. "But that wouldn't have made a great deal of sense, would it? No one would have been able to afford to bid on those sorts of pieces."

"I suppose," Mr. Adams said. "But this evening is clearly more refined...and these are the sort of exhibits I enjoy visiting most." He shifted his gaze to me, his smile growing. "Especially as they often bring the sort of people I enjoy meeting."

I knew full well that he said it so pointedly to garner a reaction out of me...and a reaction he managed to get. The color rose in my face, down my neck and up to my hairline, burning all the while. Perhaps it was silly of me to be so easily flattered, but it had been some time since I had received such obvious attention from an attractive man.

How was I supposed to reply? It had been so long since I had needed to come up with any sort of conversation that I was only drawing a blank. I could think of nothing to say, at least nothing interesting. *Who wants to discuss the weather or the state of the markets right now?* I wondered. My father and his friends would, but nobody our age cared for such things.

"You must forgive me for being so blunt, but I must say..." Mr. Adams began, his expression softening. "I heard about what happened to your uncle. Terrible, absolutely terrible. I'm glad they found the monster responsible."

I wondered if the rumors had included any hint of exactly who had identified the responsible party. As far as I knew, my name had been kept quiet and that was how I wanted it to stay. Certainly, my parents wouldn't want my involvement known. The entire matter had caused more than enough scandal.

Luckily, I saw no sign in Mr. Adams' face that he knew anything specific. Instead, the genuine sympathy I saw in his gaze soothed my nerves. "Thank you," I said. "It was a great surprise to us all."

"Adams, are you talking about the Vandegrift Hotel murder?" asked one of the young men in the group behind us.

"Yes, that's right," Mr. Adams said.

The young man, with short dark hair and a rather large gap between his front teeth, eyed me over Mr. Adams' shoulder. "My word, I'm sorry as well," he said. "I heard about it from Julia's side of the family. Apparently it was meant to look like a suicide, but it was eventually realized that the note hadn't actually been written by – "

"I think we've said enough on the subject," Mr. Adams interrupted. "We do not need to dredge up bad memories for the ladies. They've probably been through enough as it is."

"Right, of course," the other man said, nodding furiously. "My apologies."

"It's no trouble," I said, attempting an easy smile but feeling I failed.

"We should discuss more pleasant matters," Mr. Adams said. "Such as what you have thought of this exhibit thus far."

"It's...breathtaking." I settled on the word, knowing it did little justice. "I suppose I'm not as skilled in appreciating art as you must be, but I have enjoyed seeing what the artists have created. Especially Mr. Vincent Gardens."

His eyes brightened. "Mr. Gardens is a dear friend of mine," he said. "I was visiting him one afternoon at his estate on Long Island when he was painting *Even Tides.*"

He pointed over my shoulder, through another open door to the grand staircase.

"He's there, meeting with the guests and answering questions," he said. He leaned down a bit closer, dropping his voice. "Of course, if you would care to have a personal meeting with him, I would be happy to arrange such a thing after the exhibit is over this evening."

"That would be wonderful," I said.

He grinned.

He is trying to impress me, I realized. *He already wants me to like him.*

Another group of people spilled into the room, many gazing around in wonder. One of the group perked up when he spotted Mr. Adams, and hurried over toward us. "I wondered if I'd find you skulking around back here. I'm surprised you aren't out mingling."

"I am here to enjoy myself," Mr. Adams said. "Not to write an article or any of that. Why would I, when Mr. Gardens is the feature? I couldn't possibly critique him. Well, not where he might find out, at least." He and some of the others chuckled.

"Come now, you never properly take time off," said one of the women standing behind him, as she swirled the contents of her glass. "Whether or not you want to, you are always looking at the world with a critical eye."

"I suppose it's just how I am," he said with a shrug.

"He isn't critical," said the other young man with the dark hair beside her. "He is just observant, that's all. And he has standards."

"Yes, standards that hardly anyone can seem to match," said the woman. To my surprise, her eyes snapped to me, and narrowed slightly.

I looked away.

"That's quite the critique as well, you know," said the other man who had just joined the group. "What is the saying? Something about the pot calling the kettle black?"

The woman's jaw muscles clenched, but the others around them laughed.

"Opal here is a critic at the same newspaper I write for," Mr. Adams said, filling Joan and I in on the joke between them all. "She focuses mainly on theatrical performances and music, while I have found I'm happiest when I get to peruse paintings and sculptures, seeing the creations of the artists rather than the artists themselves."

"Oh..." I said. It was becoming clearer by the minute just how little I actually knew about the world these people inhabited.

"I believe I saw you at the Nutcracker performance last Christmas," Joan said, pointing at the woman called Opal. "You sat near the back with a notepad, taking extensive notes."

Mr. Adams grinned. "Wasn't that the performance you had such scathing things to say about?"

"I wasn't trying to be scathing," the woman snapped, her nose wrinkling. "That is simply what someone *said* I sounded like. It was never my intention."

"It's difficult to tell the difference sometimes," said Mr. Adams.

More chortles filled the air.

Opal turned on her heel and stomped off, her shoes clacking with purpose against the polished wood floors.

"Don't be too troubled by her," Mr. Adams said. "She often has difficulty finding anything positive to say, but you can't take it personally. Her father was a critic as well, you see, and she learned her standards from him."

"I see..." I said. "I suppose I shall have to take your word for it."

He grinned just as yet another person approached the group, this time an older gentleman. He clapped Mr. Adams on the shoulder. "Mr. Gardens would like to speak with you," he said. "Shouldn't take more than a few minutes."

"Certainly," Mr. Adams said. He turned to me, smiling. "I won't be long. Shall I come find you when I'm through?"

"Yes, that would be fine," I said.

"My sister and I will be around," Joan added, taking my arm in hers. "Looking at the exhibit."

He nodded, and hurried away after the other gentleman.

Mr. Adams' group of friends melded back together, no longer seeing the need to speak with us now that he was gone.

"I shall be back soon, too," Catherine said, beaming at me. "I need to find my father. Well done, though! I think he is already very taken with you!" She said the last part in a hurried whisper before heading off as well, back through the crowd.

Joan, as pushy as she always was, started to lead me through the crowds once again, away from Mr. Adams' friends. "She is right, you know," she said. "I think it's obvious he is interested in you. He seemed intent on garnering your approval. He's trying to figure out what you like and don't like."

"I suppose I noticed the same," I said.

She glanced over her shoulder at the group gathered there. "He even went so far as to chide one of his friends for asking too many questions. So already he's demonstrating a desire to protect you, in an attempt to maintain your respect."

"What do you think?" I asked. "Of him, that is."

She blinked at me a few times, then considered. "I'm surprised you even agreed to speak with him again. I expected you to avoid him for the rest of the evening, as much as you politely could."

"I don't see how I could do that without giving offense," I pointed out.

"When it's a complete stranger, I'm not sure how much consideration you owe him. And you were entirely unprepared to meet him anyway," she said. She tilted her head to the side, regarding me. "I would have liked more warning if it were me, as I imagine you would have too. It wouldn't be all together surprising if you brushed him off."

"I certainly would have wanted more notice, yes," I admitted. "But I do find him a little intriguing. Also..."

"Also what?" Joan asked.

"I don't know," I said. "Which is why I wanted to know what you think of him. You seem to already know about him, in a small way."

"I am aware of him, yes," she said. "He is knowledgeable and well connected."

"But what sort of man is he? What is he really like?" I asked. "That seems more pertinent right now."

"True," Joan said. "Well, I know little of that, apart from what we have seen tonight. But I will tell you that if it were me, I...wouldn't mind if he were to pursue something with me," she said. "Not that I'm saying I do want that. Catherine wished you to meet him, not me –"

"My apologies, ladies. I don't mean to interrupt, but might I have a closer look?" came a woman's voice beside us.

I turned to see a woman of some years coming up next to me, her gaze fixed on the nearby display of a gorgeous glass orb lying at rest on a golden silk pillow. Her eyes, much the same color as the green orb, swiveled around to Joan and I, the corners wrinkling as she smiled at us.

"Certainly," I said, stepping at once out of her way.

"Thank you," she said, coming to take my place in front of the exhibit. Her emerald green dress swished at her knees, perfect and shining silk like the pillow she gazed at. "It's stunning, isn't it? It amazes me how each piece so captures the title of the exhibit, each and every time."

"It reminds me of a droplet of water," I said.

She nodded. "That is precisely what I thought, as well," she said. "Tell me, were either of you here during the Night of Fire exhibit?"

Joan and I both shook our heads.

"It was earlier this summer," the woman said. "The masterpiece of the whole evening was a sculpture made of driftwood, carved in the shape of flames, which was then set ablaze by the artist himself. They extinguished the flame before the wood was entirely eaten up, leaving the charred image behind...which had changed somehow, looking like polished ebony."

"It sounds remarkable," I said.

"Entirely unconventional, as well," she added with a bit of a laugh. "My late husband, were he still with us, would have enjoyed it. This, though...it's simple and yet lovely. I much prefer art that speaks of beauty, rather than of bizarre modern ideals. Wouldn't you agree?"

"Absolutely," Joan answered, crossing her arms. "I dislike the growing admiration for abstract pieces. What, might I ask, is so special about a mash of colors left to the interpretation of the viewer?"

"I had no idea you had opinions on art," I said to my sister.

Joan rolled her eyes. "How are you to know anything if you don't ask?"

She had a point.

"My name is Bernice Milbourn, by the way," the older woman said.

"Pleased to meet you. My name is Joan Shipman and this is my sister, Sylvia," Joan said, gesturing to me.

"What a pleasure it is to see young people at an event such as this," Mrs. Milbourn said. And, if you do not mind me saying so, keeping such pleasant company, as well. Did I see you standing with a Mr. Adams'?" she asked.

"Yes, we were..." I said.

"I thought as much," she said, her smile growing. "And I heard you discussing his interest?"

This woman is awfully impertinent, I thought.

"Perhaps," Joan said, her eyebrows drawing together. "Why do you ask?"

"I don't mean to be forward, but if I might offer some advice?" she asked.

"That is very kind of you, but – " Joan said.

"That would be nice, thank you," I said, before Joan could finish her thought. She glared at me, but trailed off.

"Wonderful," Mrs. Milbourn said. "Do not second guess yourself too many times, as doubts can creep into any decision long before one is made. You said you were uncertain whether or not to pursue anything with him, given the suddenness of his appearance and your unpreparedness. I would challenge you...not every stranger you meet will remain thus."

"Well, that is simple logic," Joan said. "Of course everyone starts off as strangers."

"Precisely my point," Mrs. Milbourn said. "But what changes that? Your willingness to trust. Use wisdom, of course, be on your guard...but there will come a time where you will know, with certainty, whether or not you can trust someone. Allow yourself the time to find that moment and make the right decision."

"You are saying I should give him a chance?" I asked.

She smiled. "I am saying you will have to make a decision but also you must allow yourself the time to do so."

I heard what she meant and saw the wisdom in it... but for some reason Miles, and not Mr. Adams, was the first person to pass through my thoughts.

She gave the orb one last affectionate glance. "I suppose these are nothing more than the musings of an old woman, with her own experiences had and lessons learned," she said.

"We are appreciative of your advice, Mrs. Milbourn," I said. "Thank you."

"Well, then..." she said, glancing over her shoulder. "I suppose I should be off. My sister is around somewhere and I should not leave her for long. She begins to worry if I allow myself to become too invested in the art. Take care, you two. It was nice meeting you."

"You as well," Joan said.

"Yes, indeed," I agreed.

She gave us a wave as she departed, but she didn't make it far through the crowd. We were still watching her go when a tall, thin man bumped into her shoulder.

She staggered and looked up at him.

"My apologies," he said, reaching out to steady her.

She stared up into his face, and immediately her expression hardened. She pulled her hand quickly from his grasp and walked off.

The young man, too, slipped back into the crowd, ducking his head.

"I wonder why she was so offended at that clumsy fellow," I said.

Joan shrugged. "Who knows? She was right in what she said to you, though. You don't need to make a decision about Mr. Adams right away. You have only just met him, after all. No one is expecting you to up and marry him tomorrow."

"Well, except maybe Father if he finds out..." I said, frowning slightly.

"I think he has too much on his mind right now," Joan said. "Mother on the other hand..."

Across the distance, I saw Mrs. Milbourn again.

She had straightened near the doorway, stretching her neck. I imagined she was looking for her sister.

"She was nice," I said, watching her glance from side to side. In the midst of such a large crowd, it was no wonder she was struggling to find someone. "I appreciated her candidness."

"Of course you did," Joan said, though I couldn't tell if she was being sarcastic. "Come on. Let's see if we can find Catherine. Maybe she will have seen Mr. Adams. Or maybe he will come to find us."

"Maybe…" I said, glancing over my shoulder for Mrs. Milbourn.

She was gone.

Joan and I wandered past a few more of the glass sculptures before I finally caught a glimpse of Mr. Adams entering the room once again. He grinned as his eyes fell on me.

In that instant, a terrible, blood-curdling scream filled the gallery.

3

"What in the world?" Joan asked even as people around us began to rush about, looking for the source of the scream. "Is that part of the exhibit?"

Something deep down told me it had absolutely nothing to do with the exhibit...and everything to do with something gone horribly wrong.

A few more screams burst out of the crowd, this time from near the doorway back into the main part of the gallery.

"She's been attacked!" came a male voice, rising with hysterics.

"What happened?" asked another man.

"Run for your lives!" cried yet a third person, this time a woman.

I staggered as someone collided with me, sending

me sprawling into one of the white pedestals beside me. I gasped as the perfect, clear sphere shook and rocked. I reached out and took it in my hands before it sailed off the pillow and shattered against the floor.

More people hurried away from the doorway, while others lingered there, seemingly frozen in place. An indistinguishable shape of emerald green lay on the floor, and my heart jumped into my throat.

That couldn't be... No, surely it isn't –

"She – She's been killed!" a woman burst out beside us as she and her husband hurried away. "How could that possibly have happened?"

"Who could have done such a thing?" asked a man following close behind.

"Pardon me, sir, but what's happened?" Joan asked, stepping out in front of the gentleman.

"I – I don't rightly know," the man answered, wiping his broad forehead with a handkerchief. "A woman has fallen over there and people are claiming she's dead." He started away. "I'm sorry, but I must find my family."

"Surely it – " I said, my palms suddenly slick and heart palpitating. "It couldn't be – "

"Are you both all right?"

I looked up at a familiar face.

"Mr. Adams," Joan said. "Thank goodness. Do you know what's going on?"

"It's still unfolding but we should get you both out

of here," he said, ushering us both with a hand against our backs.

He steered us behind the pedestal, nearer to the windows.

"That isn't a person over there, is it?" I asked. "On the floor?"

Mr. Adams said nothing, but his gaze lingered over in the doorway that people moved away from. "Don't look," he said. "It will only distress you."

"What is it?" Joan asked. "Who is it?"

"We don't know," Mr. Adams said.

I stopped, a gap appearing between the people standing over her, allowing me to see quite clearly that it was, in fact, Mrs. Milbourn…so easily identifiable by the emerald green dress she wore.

My heart pounded as my mind sucked in the scene like dry ground drinking in rain. She lay sprawled on her stomach, her arms bent at odd angles…and the handle of a knife sticking out from between her shoulder blades.

"Come along…" Mr. Adams said, seeing what I had now seen. His tone, gentle and calm, urged me on.

He brought us into one of the back rooms of the gallery, away from the gruesome scene. It seemed we weren't the only ones who had thought to put as much distance between ourselves and the dead woman as possible.

"I'm sorry this is the best I can do right now," he

said. “I have sent some of my friends out to telephone the police, though I imagine we weren’t the only ones.”

“How long will that take?” Joan asked.

“Hopefully not long,” Mr. Adams said. “Will you be all right in here while I go and try to find the rest of my group?”

“Yes, we should be,” I said.

“What if the murderer is in here?” Joan asked.

Mr. Adams stiffened. His brow furrowed and he looked around. “Maybe it would be best for me to stay here, then. Or maybe you should come with me.”

I, likewise, didn’t like the idea of staying in the room where the killer might be…but that wasn’t what troubled me most.

“We should be all right for a few minutes,” I said. “We must find Miss Catherine, as well. I want to make sure she is safe.”

Mr. Adams nodded. “Very well. Then I will meet you back here in just a few minutes.”

Joan looked at me, her brow furrowing. “Why didn’t you want to – ”

“Joan, you and I were the last people to speak with her,” I said, grabbing her hands, drawing her close so that she would hear my frantic whispers. “What are we supposed to do?”

She blinked at me, her expression falling. She looked around, eyeing those nearest to us, before licking her lips and returning her attention to me. “…

And?" she asked, her face hardening. "What would that have to do with anything?"

"Joan..." I murmured, my heart fluttering in my chest. "What if someone finds out? Surely someone would have seen her with us, and – "

"Calm down," Joan said, laying her hands on my arms. But she couldn't deceive me; her hands shook just as much as my own. "We cannot afford to lose our heads here."

"But she – she – " I said, my breath catching in my chest, causing quick, shallow gasps. "She's dead now, and she was only just speaking with us – "

"All right," Joan said in a hiss. "We had *nothing* to do with it. Not a thing!"

"I know!" I said. "But something happened after she walked away!"

But what? I wondered. *What, or who, had done this?*

"Obviously, it was no accident," I said, my mind racing faster than my words could keep up with. "I mean, no one could have been carrying a knife around in the open and just *happened* to stab her in the back – "

"Sylvia – " Joan said, slapping her hand over my mouth. Her deep blue eyes blazed, as she willed me not to speak any further.

I swallowed the rest of the questions that permeated my brain, and nodded.

She lowered her hand, looking around. "You won't

say anything, to anyone. We had nothing to do with it. We *know* that."

"What if she told us something important?" I asked. "It might not have seemed that way to us, but it's possible she said something that could tell us who the killer was."

Joan's brow furrowed. "What does that matter to us?" she asked. "We have no involvement, and we should *keep it that way*."

"But these are the sorts of questions Miles would be asking..." I said in a murmur.

Her eyes narrowed further. "What did you say?" she asked.

"It's – " I said, hesitating. "It's nothing."

She continued to stare at me, her gaze burning into the side of my cheek as we stood there.

"Everyone, please, settle down."

I lifted my head, finding a man who likely was around our father's age standing just inside the doorway. Catherine slipped into the room, but lingered nearby, and at once I could see the resemblance.

"Is that her father?" Joan asked.

"I think so," I said. "How long has it been since I saw him?"

Clearly, it had been quite some time, as he looked almost unrecognizable. A man who had once been svelte and tall had morphed into a pear-shaped figure with more than one chin. He surveyed the room, his arms sweeping outward.

"I understand that many of you will have questions, none of which I can answer at this time," he said, and with each word, I recognized his voice more and more. It must have been ten years since I had heard it, and suddenly I was feeling as if I were a child all over again. "The police have already begun to arrive and are looking into the matter. They have asked me to keep everyone here for questioning – "

"What?"

"You can't keep us here!"

"We've done nothing wrong!"

The outcries echoed around the room, swallowing each other up as they burst out.

Mr. Waters held his hands up for silence, and slowly the others around us quieted. "I ask for your patience," he said, his tone as firm as his gaze. "This is a great tragedy that has happened on my watch, and I will not allow some monster to come in here and attack such a beloved member of this community."

Nervous glances were exchanged, and the tension rose to palpable levels. *The person who did this very likely walked through the same rooms we did, likely stood beside us and we had no idea...*I realized.

"Now I know many of you personally, and ask as your friend that you remain here and allow the police to do their jobs," he continued. "This is...a terrible thing that's happened, but it has happened, and we must deal with it as swiftly as possible. Once you have been cleared, then you are free to be on your way. Until there has been some time for the police to assess the situation, please remain here. I will have the staff bring any of the drinks and food that we can find."

It might not have entirely diffused the situation, but it certainly seemed to take some of the pressure off. People began to turn to one another, the atmosphere swarming with the sound of hushed whispers and some tears, reminding me of a swarm of bees.

My head swam, and I had to reach out to the wall beside me for support.

"Careful with that," Joan said, reaching down to scoop the orb from my arms. She cradled it like a baby, looking around. "The last thing we need is to be known as the last to speak with Mrs. Milbourn *and* shatter a priceless exhibit piece..."

"Right..." I said.

It mattered little to me that she held it, since she seemed to have a better grip on the situation than I did. At least, she appeared to have more control, as my heart continued to pound uncomfortably inside my ribs every time I saw a police officer walk in or out of the room.

They're coming for us! I thought each time one of the officers passed through the room, and each time, they would stroll right past.

Catherine disappeared with her father, which hardly surprised me. "It might be for the best," I added, after sharing this observation with Joan. "I'm not sure what she would think if she found out we had spoken with Mrs. Milbourn."

"It's hardly a crime to speak with someone," Joan pointed out, but I could see she was also uneasy over how it might appear. "I wonder if anyone else saw anything..." she said, absently running her thumb over the sphere, her gaze fixed on the doorway which was now blocked by a pair of policemen. From what we had been able to understand, they were beginning to clean up the scene.

"I don't know..." I said. "I certainly hope someone saw it all."

She turned her gaze to me, still scrutinizing. "You went through this before, when Uncle Walter died. How much would they need to go on in order to find who did this?" she asked.

"What do you mean?" I asked.

"Just as I said," she said, her eyes narrowing further. "You did the investigating before and found out who killed our uncle. How did you learn the truth? What about the night Uncle Walter died helped you figure it out?"

I pondered her words for a moment, retracing my own steps in my mind. "Well," I started slowly. "The most obvious choice was his fiancé, at least at first," I said. "When we ruled her out, then I wondered if it might have been Father, given a conversation I had overheard between him and someone else – " I stopped, and looked around.

"What?" Joan asked. "What is it?"

I blinked a few times, a pair of memories colliding with one another. "Joan, maybe we are looking at this wrong," I said. "We were the last to *speak* with her, that much I am almost positive of – but do you remember that man who bumped into her just as she walked away from us?"

She frowned. "I think so," she said. "Why?"

"I wonder if he might know something about it," I said.

"What made you think of that?" she asked.

"Looking back on it, I focused on the wrong part of Father's conversation with Mr. Morrow," I said. "I suppose it has taught me to examine those sorts of moments from both sides. Namely, this one where what I thought was the truth might very well not be."

Her eyes widened. "Then what should we do?" she asked. "Should we go and tell the police about him?"

I looked around. "If it would help this all be resolved faster, then yes, I think we should."

Joan took my hand, and tucking the orb beneath her arm, strode toward the doorway with me immediately behind her.

We were drawing nearer to the police when Mr.

Waters stepped back into the room. "I have been asked to inform you that you are all to follow me and leave the exhibit hall," he said. "A more thorough investigation is to take place, and they do not wish to do so with as many people here as there are."

My heart skipped as the hordes behind us moved as if in unison, all swarming toward the door. *We need to find someone to tell!* I thought.

"Joan, we need to speak with Mr. Waters," I said.

"Right," she said, veering to the left to cross his path before he disappeared.

"Mr. Waters!" I exclaimed, stepping out in front of him.

The father of my friend stopped and regarded me with a blank stare. "I'm sorry, Miss, but I cannot help you right now. As you can see, I am very busy at the moment – "

"Mr. Waters, I'm Catherine's friend, and – " I said.

"Yes, it's very nice to see you again, I'm sure," he said, his eyes falling anywhere *but* on me. "Oh, is that one of our pieces? Thank you very much, I will take that."

Without preempt, he took the orb from Joan's arms, and walked off in a hurry.

I stared after him, my heart sinking.

"Let's find one of those officers," Joan said, taking my arm and starting off again.

We followed the exiting crowd once more, my

mind reeling as a sense of de ja vu washed over me. *How similar this is to the exodus from the hotel,* I thought, recalling the night of my uncle's death.

A number of sheets and other fabrics had been strewn across the floor. My stomach rolled over as I realized it was the precise place where Mrs. Milbourn had been lying. She had been moved, mercifully, but I did wonder where they had taken her body.

I turned away, closing my eyes as Joan continued to lead me. *I am sorry, Mrs. Milbourn,* I thought. *Perhaps if we had continued our conversation, if I hadn't been so consumed with my thoughts, we might have delayed your demise or prevented it all together. Was it an accident? Were you simply at the wrong place at the wrong time?*

I frowned as we left the room.

Or were you the target? Did someone have it out for you from the very beginning of the night? That thought troubled me all the more.

A policeman stood near the front doors.

"Excuse me, sir," I said, lingering just inside the door.

The officer blew the whistle clamped between his teeth, the shrill sound sending shivers down my spine. He waved his arm in a sweeping motion, as if wafting smoke out the doors. He said nothing, continuing instead to direct the traffic of the people flowing from the exhibit hall.

"Pardon me, officer?" I asked, a bit louder.

Joan turned around out on the sidewalk, looking wildly about her until she saw me still up near the doors. "Sylvia, what are you – "

"Sir, please," I said, stepping into his line of sight. "I believe I might be able to help you with that woman's death," I said.

He finally looked down at me. "You and the last four people who stopped," he said, his whistle murmuring with every *S* sound. "And none of it was helpful."

"Yes, but I saw someone bump into the dead woman just a few moments before she was killed – " I said.

He glared at me, pulling the whistle from his lips. "Unless you have something a bit more concrete, then I'm afraid that means nothing," he said. "All we have managed to find are trivial facts, nothing that would be at all out of place on an ordinary evening. But as someone has turned up dead, suddenly *everyone* thinks they know something."

I blinked at him, stunned for a moment. "I'm sorry, but the look she gave the man who collided with her makes me wonder if – "

"I don't have time for theories about suspicious *looks*," the policeman said. "Please move along."

Joan reappeared at my side. "You don't even wish to hear what she has to say?" she asked.

"No," the officer said, quite plainly. "If you want,

you can leave your name so we can contact you if we have any further questions."

Joan huffed, taking me by the arm. "Thank you, officer. We will leave it to you, then."

He said nothing as Joan pulled me down the sidewalk, away from the exhibit.

"Wait," I said. "I should leave my name – "

"I think it would be best if you leave this all behind this time, Sylvia," Joan said. "It's clear they don't want any help."

I hesitated, glancing over my shoulder.

"Maybe they've already learned what they needed to," Joan said. "Which would be a good thing, right? Then they wouldn't need to talk to us in the first place."

"Yes, that would be good..." I said, my voice drifting off. Still, I couldn't shake the idea that something wasn't right. "I just hope there wasn't anything she told us that could have helped."

"Doubtful," Joan said. "It was a perfectly ordinary conversation, and she might have exchanged similar remarks with many other people this evening. And as I said, maybe they already found who did this. Or maybe that officer just has no interest in helping his colleagues. I *imagine* if his superior were to hear, he would be furious to learn someone who might have evidence was turned away."

"I suppose we could always go to – " I began.

"No," Joan said, turning on me. "No, we are leaving this to them. *You* are leaving this to them. Even if you had a hand in solving our uncle's murder – all right, you were the one who figured it out in the end – that doesn't mean you need to be invested in this one as well."

"You're right," I said. *...Though I still can't help but feel that we might have been able to help...* "To think that we might have been the ones to hear her last words..."

Joan wrinkled her nose, taking my hand in hers and starting back down the sidewalk. "Yes, well, nothing we can do about that, is there?" she asked. "Nothing we can do about it at all."

I couldn't exactly argue with her there.

"She took all that time to give us advice, to encourage us," I said.

"Let's not rehash it," she said. "To be honest, I'm not certain my stomach can handle it."

I nodded, and we continued on.

She flagged a taxicab with a wave of her arm, and soon we were on our way. We didn't speak the whole way home, and as we climbed the front steps to our house, Joan turned to me.

"We have now experienced this twice, both times together," she said, her blue eyes alight. "At least this time we can have some peace, knowing it had nothing to do with us or our family."

"That's true," I said.

"Come on," she said. "We should get inside – "

I took hold of the back of her sleeve, halting her ascent.

She glanced at me over her shoulder.

"Can we…just keep this between us?" I asked.

She blinked, her expression blank. "Everyone is going to wonder why we are home early," she said.

"I know," I said. I didn't want to think of Miles hearing yet another story about a murder. I had hardly recovered from Uncle Walter's death, let alone what I had learned from that newspaper clipping I'd found in Miles' room. If he were to hear about what happened tonight, I could only assume he would take the first opportunity to ask me about it, and maybe even offer to help.

I didn't know what I would do if he did.

Joan sighed. "Very well," she said. "I can just tell them that all the excitement was short-lived. Not a complete lie, I suppose."

"Thank you," I said.

We passed through the door, and I couldn't remember a time that I had been happier to be home. The only thing that would have been better was if I knew for sure that Mrs. Milbourn's killer had been caught…and that I wouldn't have anything to do with it.

4

It seemed that every other year Sutton Place experienced the season's first snow fall before the first of December. This year, it evidently wanted to show up on the tenth of November.

"I should have expected it, too," I told Joan over a breakfast of hot porridge with maple syrup and cream. "As cold as it's been since the middle of October."

"I've never been able to understand why you despise it so much," she replied, sipping her coffee, her cup delicately balanced between the tips of her fingers. She couldn't fool me; she relished the heat seeping into her undoubtedly cold hands. "The first snow fall is so romantic." She gazed at the pair of windows on the other side of the table from us. Flakes the size of buttons tumbled silently from the sky.

Romantic...cold...very different in my opinion.

"Oh, I do wish we could go to our country home for Christmas this year," said Mother from her seat beside Father. She fluttered her eyelashes at him, preening like a hen. "Can I not convince you to change your mind?"

Father folded the top of the newspaper down just enough so that he could eye Mother over it. "I have already told you, the cost alone would be impractical this year," he said before disappearing behind the thick paper covered in tiny ink letters.

My heart sank. In truth, going to our country home felt like precisely what we needed right now. I would have liked nothing more than to go and spend the entire winter there. *Perhaps Joan and I could go by ourselves, leave Mother and Father here so that Father can take care of whatever it is he needs to. Some time in the quiet would be good, away from the city, away from the difficulties –*

"Miles, this weather must be a shock for you," Father said. "I have been to London a few times in the winter, and you hardly have snow there, do you?"

Miles stepped away from the wall beside the window, and I couldn't politely ignore him any longer. His blonde hair lay swept back over his head, clean and not a strand out of place. He bowed his head. "Yes sir, that is correct," he said. "And I must agree with Miss Sylvia. I much prefer the warmer months."

Father laughed, which surprised me. When was the last time I had heard him laugh? Genuinely?

"This snow won't last," Father said with a gesture toward the windows. "It's too soon. The ground is too warm. It will melt, and the city shall be back to normal..." His voice trailed off, and his brief smile faded like an anchor sinking below the surface of the river. "It shall be back to normal."

I recognized the weariness in his tone and knew full well that he was no longer talking about the weather.

Miles glanced down the table at me, and when he met my gaze, he smiled.

I looked away, snatching my coffee cup off the table. It sloshed out onto my hands, but I ignored the searing of the hot liquid by biting my tongue as I drew the cup to my lips.

"One moment..." Father said, drawing the paper closer to his face. "What was the name of the art gallery the two of you went to last evening?"

My eyes snapped to Joan, widening. *Why hadn't I thought about this?*

"I don't rightly remember," Joan said. "It was near Central Park, that much I do know."

"This paper says that a woman died there last night," he said. "Though I imagine you left before anything like that happened?"

Joan's head swiveled around to me, and I groaned

internally. *You might as well have shouted from the rooftops that we know full well what he is talking about.*

"Someone died?" Mother asked, aghast. "Is that true?"

Joan stared at me, her eyes widening.

Well, it wasn't likely that we could lie to them, not when asked so directly.

"*Last night, amidst the group of gallery attendees, Mrs. Bernice Milbourn was attacked and killed. It is unclear how such a thing could occur when there were more than a hundred people in attendance, and no one seems to have seen anything of significance. Mrs. Milbourn was a frequent visitor to the gallery, and a generous donor, often giving great amounts in order to help the gallery reach desired milestones for refurbishments. It is a mystery why such a generous woman was the target of such a gruesome murder.*"

Father lowered the paper, his piercing gaze fixing on Joan and me.

I ducked my head. I knew *that* look.

"Well...we didn't wish to worry anyone," Jo said, shrugging, her palms upturned. "We know you already have so much to deal with right now, Father, that we – "

"You knew?" Father asked. "My word, girl. How could you not have said so sooner?"

"Did you see what happened?" Mother asked. "Were either of you in any danger?"

Joan gave me a quick, sidelong look.

I said nothing, shrugging and shaking my head.

She clearly took it as confirmation that I was all right with whatever she had to say, as I had thought she would. "We just barely saw it happen," she said. "And there was this terrible scream! Everyone turned just in time to see the old woman's body fall to the floor."

Mother gasped as any good audience member would.

Joan nodded. "Next we saw, as people ran away from her, a knife had been planted squarely in her back."

"Oh, my word!" Mother exclaimed.

"How is that possible?" Father asked. "The article said there were over a hundred people there."

"There certainly were," Joan said. "And that's the mystery, isn't it? No one has any idea who did this, or how they accomplished it. One minute she was alive, talking enthusiastically, embracing and loving her life, and then the next – she was dead."

"What happened after that?" Mother asked, hiding her mouth behind her hand.

"The police arrived, and herded us all like cattle to the back rooms of the gallery, where they came one by one to speak with some of the guests," Joan said.

That's not at all how it happened, I thought, but knew she wouldn't appreciate being interrupted, even in her embellishments.

"No one could explain it. It's as if a ghost showed up in our midst and attacked her," Joan said. "The police were baffled, so much so that they could do nothing more than take their frustration out on guests as they marched us out the front doors. I suppose they cleared us out to look for evidence."

Father's head swung in my direction. "Is this true?" he asked.

I blinked at him. "What do you mean?"

His expression hardened. "What she is talking about. Did this all really happen when you both were there last night?"

I couldn't be certain why he was asking me when Joan had just told him the basics of what had occurred, with a bit more color than might have been the truth. "Yes, it did," I said. "No one saw anything or knows what happened."

"Obviously it must have been one of the people there to see the exhibit," Joan said. "Which is curious. I wonder how they will find out who did it?"

"Isn't Mr. Waters the one who owns that gallery?" Father asked.

I perked up. "Yes, he is," I said. "He was there last night."

Father shook his head. "I don't envy him all that mess. One can only hope the police were able to find something so they can put this business in the past as swiftly as possible."

"Oh, then I wonder if Catherine has heard anything new?" Joan asked.

"I don't know," I said.

"Nothing happened out of the ordinary before the woman died?" Father asked. "That seems terribly unlikely."

"Well, nothing out of the ordinary perhaps, but we saw her bump into someone as she was walking off last night," Joan said. "And she gave him the most disgusted look."

"Who was it?" Mother asked.

"We have no idea," Joan said. "And – "

But her words were lost to me as I considered Catherine Waters, and whether or not she might know who the man was that bumped into Mrs. Milbourn last night, and what might have caused Mrs. Milbourn to look at him with such disgust.

I made up my mind after breakfast to go and see Catherine, to tell her what I had witnessed. *I can tell her, and she can tell her father. This way, it will be out of my control and in the hands of someone who can really do something. That is better for us all.*

Joan had plans for lunch with some friends, and as such, could not accompany me. I deemed it worthwhile to take a taxicab down to Catherine's house instead of asking Miles to drive. I hadn't seen him since the day before, and still struggled to know what I should or shouldn't say to him. I couldn't even *look* at him without thinking about his mysterious past...

"OH, how pleased I am to see you," Catherine said when she entered the sunroom of her home. The Waters family lived about a mile north of us, nearer to the gallery and the center of the city. They owned a handsome brownstone two stories higher than ours, with substantially more space for Catherine and her six other siblings. "I had hoped I would have the chance to catch up with you after what happened last night."

She asked me to take a seat on the long chaise beside the window. Grey light streaked in through the wall of windows behind us, not the glorious afternoon sun we had often enjoyed in the height of summer. Once again, I grumbled in my heart about the coming bitterness and cold and lamented the lack of blue skies and swirling white clouds.

She sat on the matching seat beside me, laying her head back. "You must forgive me," she went on. "I am positively exhausted after everything. Father wouldn't let me out of his sight after what happened and we were unable to leave the gallery until almost four in the morning."

"Four?" I repeated. "Why so late?"

"The police were looking for something, *anything* that might give them information," she said with a heavy sigh. She stared up at the ceiling, her wide eyes sweeping the pressed copper tiles overhead. "Apart from the knife in her back, they found nothing. They knew that they had likely sent the culprit home unknowingly, but by that time, it was already too late."

"I'm sorry to hear that," I said.

"It isn't your fault," she said with a wave. "It isn't as if *you* had something to do with any of this."

"No, certainly not..." I said. "But Joan and I might have been the last ones to speak with Mrs. Milbourn before her death."

Catherine sat up, her eyes fixing on me. "Really?" she asked. "How? When? What did she say?"

I held up my hands defensively. "She said nothing of great value," I said, and repeated what I could remember of our conversation.

"She only gave you advice?" Catherine asked. She heaved a sigh, lying back down against the chaise. "I suppose that is of no great surprise," she said. "She had no way of knowing what was about to happen, and so it makes sense that her last conversation would have been about trivial matters." She furrowed her brow. "So it seems she really had no warning that she was about to die."

"Not from anything she told us, anyway," I said. "Though Joan and I were perfect strangers to her. I don't suspect she would have shared any personal concerns with us."

"Perhaps not..." Catherine said. "There has to be something else, though, right? Someone most certainly had a bone to pick with her if they were willing to attack her in the midst of such a large group."

"I imagine so, yes..." I said. "That is why I am here, in part."

"Why?" Catherine asked.

"Well...I felt strangely responsible in some way, because Joan and I had spoken with her last night, but something else odd happened, as well. I tried to tell one of the police officers, but he would have nothing to do with insignificant facts."

"What happened?" Catherine asked, propping herself up on one elbow.

"As Mrs. Milbourn walked away from us last night, a young man bumped into her. I assume it was entirely by accident, as there were so many people in those exhibit halls, but Joan and I both glimpsed her expression, and..."

"What? And what?" Catherine questioned.

"I...can't quite explain it," I said. "Apart from the fact that Mrs. Milbourn looked...furious."

"That is interesting," Catherine said. "What did this young man look like?"

"Tall, thin..." I said, trying my best to recall. "He

wore a hat and had a bit of a crooked nose. Sharp features, dark hair – "

"Did he have somewhat large ears?" Catherine asked. "Reminding you of a bat?"

I straightened. "That's a rather good description."

Catherine rolled her eyes, lying down on her back again. "That's Julian Steeles, without a doubt," she said. "And it's little wonder that she gave him a nasty look." She sighed. "Oh, I had really hoped you might have something I could share with Papa."

My heart sank. "I'm sorry," I said, sheepish. "I take it her dislike of him is already known, then?"

"*Everyone* dislikes him that knows him," Catherine said. She clicked her tongue. "He is pretentious and proud. All he knows how to do is portraits. He might be very good at it, but it's difficult to appreciate an artist who can only seem to do one thing." She sighed.

"Something tells me there is...more?" I asked, watching her fingers drum against the arm of her dress.

"The fool has offered proposals to me at least half a dozen times, but all of them in complete jest," she said, rolling her eyes. "He takes no woman seriously and thinks monogamous relationships outdated."

"He sounds..." I began, but was unable to find the right word.

"He's harmless enough, but irritating," she continued. "Ever since he was commissioned for the portrait of a popular senator, he believes he deserves all praise from all artists. It was what put him in the eye of the art community, and he has allowed it to go straight to his head."

"I see," I said.

"Mrs. Milbourn, like so many others who had any sort of association with the gallery, found him annoying. A bit of a pest to some of the more prominent artists, or so Papa has told me," she said.

"So you think Mrs. Milbourn's reaction upon seeing him was nothing more than annoyance?" I asked.

She shrugged. "It's possible and quite likely," she said. "I will mention it to my father, of course, but there were so many people in that room – and you didn't see him produce a knife? Didn't see him go after her?"

I shook my head, some of the worry dissipating. "No, they went separate ways in the crowd," I said. "And that had to have been...well, at least a few minutes before she was attacked."

Catherine nodded. "As I said, I will tell my father, but I can't imagine it will amount to anything."

"I do wish I could have given you more useful information," I said. "I feel so terrible about what happened."

Catherine's face split into a sad sort of smile. "I understand," she said. "Mrs. Milbourn was a phenomenal artist, though she never once talked about it. All she ever would do was smile when someone complimented her."

"What sort of paintings did she do?" I asked.

"Watercolor," Catherine said, and somehow, that made perfect sense to me. "Which reminds me..." She hopped up, and led me back through the sunroom to the hallway along the back of the house.

We stopped in front of a lovely piece, depicting a pond dotted with water lilies, surrounded by a Weeping Willow and a pair of pines. Simple, but it made me feel so...

"...Peaceful," I finally said.

"Isn't it, though?" she asked.

"I take it this is a piece by Mrs. Milbourn?" I asked.

Catherine nodded. "Indeed."

"I can see why she was popular," I said.

"Yes," Catherine said. "It's a pity that so few knew her name as of late."

"How so?" I asked.

"Some of the younger artists found her style antiquated," Catherine said. "For whatever reason, she had fallen out of vogue with them."

"That's a pity," I said. "If the rest of her work is anything like this piece, then surely it could be appreciated by anyone."

"You know what I think?" she asked, crossing her arms. "I think they were jealous of her. I know Julian Steeles certainly would have been, given her early success that he has yet to experience. She used to have many exhibits in her name, featuring nothing but her pieces."

"I imagine that would make many people jealous," I said.

"You aren't wrong about that," she said.

I started off a short while later, seeing Catherine waving to me through the window near the front door. I returned her wave, thankful for her friendship and honesty. It struck me as the taxi pulled away that Mrs. Milbourn's legacy would live on, in bits and pieces of her art hanging with pride in the homes of those who appreciated her creativity.

It saddened me further, however, to think that she was no longer around. Who knew how she might have lived had her life not been stolen from her? Perhaps she would have done up some glorious paintings that would have changed the minds of all the young artists.

I frowned, catching a glimpse of my own reflection in the window of the back of the car. How was it that someone who was so talented had wound up with a knife in her back?

And the better question than even that was...why?

5

I half believed I should visit our family physician to have my head checked when the next morning I found myself on the way to Julian Steeles' studio in the Upper East Side. I had made the mad decision over breakfast, as I realized that I wouldn't be able to put this behind me until I found out who had committed the crime. I couldn't explain it, but I felt that I owed it to the dead woman.

I had no idea where to begin. I only knew my mind continued to drift back to Julian Steeles. I had understood everything Catherine had explained to me, but it didn't sit right with me. I had seen that look on Mrs. Milbourn's face when he had bumped into her, had known that it meant *more*. Something deep within told me it had to have something to do with her death. If he knew *anything*, then I had to find it out. Her death couldn't simply fade into history without so much as a murmur.

And after everything I went through trying to find my uncle's killer, I know just how tough it is to have to live through such a mystery, to simply not know what happened or why. If I can, I will give the truth to Mrs. Milbourn's family...even if they never know it comes from me. As the last person to speak with her in life, it feels like a sign of some sort, like the responsibility is mine.

I stared up at the towering skyscrapers over my head, some a dozen stories tall in this part of the city. Guilt wrestled with my worry, fighting for a primary spot, as I thought about how I had purposely avoided Joan before leaving the house. I knew she would have seen right through my motives, questioned me and wondered what in the world I was doing. She would have called me foolish for going, and now that the car began to slow down, I realized she might very well be right.

I stepped out, staring up at the brick structure. Music hummed through an open window nearby, piano keys being gently tickled. From a building across the street, I heard a woman singing, a lovely soprano with a trill in her voice that sent shivers down my spine.

There's no doubt this is a neighborhood for artists, I realized.

I headed toward the building. It had taken a few

telephone calls for me to dig up the public information but I had managed to learn that this was the address where I would find a certain Mr. Julian Steeles.

I had tried to avoid Miles this morning. Part of me thought his presence might have been good in this situation, and yet I still found I didn't know what to say to him. Every time I saw him, all I could think about was the woman who might have been his wife, and how she was now dead. It was as if he was a stranger all over again, and all I had known about him felt like a lie.

However, that hadn't stopped him from springing upon me just before I had exited the house, asking if I required the car. I had planned to hail a taxi on the street but could find no excuse to do so when he was right there, expecting to drive me wherever I needed to go.

"Shall I accompany you inside, Miss Sylvia?" he asked now, closing the car door behind me. "Or did you wish to speak with this man alone?"

"That was my plan," I said, ducking my head as he passed by me. "But now that you suggest it, perhaps it would be best if you come up with me. Father might make some sort of fuss, if he hears of my visiting a stranger alone. Artists have a reputation, after all."

Miles didn't question it, though I could see in his eyes that he was certainly curious about my purpose here. He may have noticed I was doing all I could these past several days to stay out of his way, and while he didn't challenge me on that, I suspected questions about my reasons would likely come eventually.

Or...maybe they wouldn't. I supposed only time would tell.

He started toward the building, pulling open the front door to a handsome and bright foyer beyond. A plaque on the wall informed us that Mr. Steeles' studio resided on the third floor. Miles gave me a gesture to indicate that I might begin the climb first.

In truth, I was relieved that he had suggested joining me. I might have allowed my feelings about Mrs. Milbourn's death to spur me into action, along with the guilt, but that didn't mean I needed to act in a foolhardy way. If this artist truly was dangerous, who knew how he might react to my visit?

I reached the top of the landing and waited for Miles to resume his place in front of me. He asked nothing as he walked past, and made his way to the door across from us. It was only one of two doors in the narrow hall before the stairway wound up again.

Miles approached the door and gave it a firm series of knocks, before waiting.

"One moment, please," came a reply in a sing-song sort of tone.

Miles gave me a sidelong look, his brows lifting.

I shrugged. I hadn't met the man the night before, nor hardly knew anything about him. I could only hope Miles would go along with the story I had concocted in my head. *It isn't as if he is going to challenge me, not really,* I thought as I heard footsteps approaching from the other side of the door.

It swung inward, and the same tall, bat-like man stood opposite us. He was even taller than I remembered, a bit spindly like a wiry tree. He gave Miles and me a sweeping smile, brimming with confidence as he surveyed me down the length of his nose. "Well, *hello* there, Miss. What can I do for *you*?"

"This is Miss Shipman," Miles said quickly. "I am her father's personal aid and have accompanied her here because she has a request of you."

I glanced at him. I had said nothing specific to him, yet he had deduced that there had to be a reason why I wanted to come all the way out here, and had offered a suitably vague explanation. Worry gnawed at my insides. *Once again, he is far more perceptive than I would care to consider.* "Yes, I do have a request," I said. "I was hoping you would have some availability in the next few weeks?"

Mr. Steeles leaned against the doorway, his smile growing. "Availability, you say? What sort of availability are we talking about?"

My cheeks flushed. This wasn't going how I had imagined. "I am not speaking of personal availability of course, but was hoping I might commission you for a portrait."

Mr. Steeles' expression didn't change, like a coy cat trying to tease its owner. I could almost see the swishing tail. "I would assume nothing else," he said with a bit of a chuckle. He spun gracefully on his heels, making me wonder if he had not dabbled in dance at some point in time, and strode into his studio.

The first things I noticed were the windows along both the western and eastern walls. His studio stretched the full length of the building, which given the exposed rafters and beams over our heads, made me realize it must have been a warehouse at some point in time. It was nothing beautiful to look at, but the room was awash with brilliant, natural light, even as grey as the late autumn had been.

There were paintings scattered around the room. They hung from the walls, they rested in easel frames, they lay upon long, smooth tables of untreated wood. Color burst from each of them, brilliant and stark against the drab surroundings.

The air smelled of oil paints and turpentine. Candles flickered in mismatched candlesticks and hung overhead from low chandeliers.

I had never been to an artist's private studio, but this place certainly seemed to be precisely what I would have imagined it to be.

"Shall I show you around?" Mr. Steeles asked.

"I would be honored," I said.

"Wonderful," he said, crossing the room to me in

only a few long strides. "Over here are some of my more recent portraits. You might recognize a few of them..."

He gestured to a trio set in easels by the windows, and I gasped.

"That is the Platt family, isn't it?" I asked.

"Oh, you *know* them, do you?" he asked, and chuckled. "My, my. I should have known a woman so lovely was surely well connected."

"I don't know them personally, but my father does," I said.

"How interesting," he said. "And over here are my newest clients." These were faces I didn't know, but they were all very beautiful women.

"They seem so lifelike," I said, surveying them. "These are so different from some of the pieces I saw the other night at the exhibit."

"The exhibit?" he asked, his tone cooling a few degrees. "Are you talking about the *Sea of Glass* exhibit?"

I froze, wondering if I might have shown my hand too early. "Yes, I am," I said. "Were you there, as well?"

"I was indeed," he said.

I wondered if it meant anything that he hadn't lied or attempted to conceal that he had been present.

He looked away from me, leaving my side to walk over to one of his work stations along the back wall, comprised of a cabinet filled with jars of paint, brushes, and fresh canvas and paper. "I assume you heard what happened?" he asked.

I hardly knew him but the tone he used seemed... cautious. As if he wanted to see precisely how much I knew. "I did, yes..." I said. *What do I say? How do I get him to keep talking?*

"It's such a shame," he said, picking up a few brushes scattered on the table beside the open cabinet, likely left out to dry. "Mrs. Milbourn...what a gift to the art community she was."

I perked up. He was willing to discuss her? Perhaps this wouldn't be so difficult after all. *If I can get him to give me something to go on, then maybe I could really help solve this.*

I glanced over toward the door. Miles stood there near the wall, his eyes fixed squarely on me. I had known him long enough to know his attention likely had not shifted since we entered the room. But like a good butler, he had melded into the background, undetectable to almost anyone not paying attention. His gaze hardened a bit when I met it, and try as I might, I couldn't tell if he was warning me. Now that the topic of Mrs. Milbourn had been addressed, he surely would have figured out my purpose for being here. Would he approve? Or would he think I was meddling in something dangerous?

"I have heard from my dear friend, Catherine

Waters, that Mrs. Milbourn was a remarkable woman, a pillar of the art world," I said.

Mr. Steeles sighed heavily, shaking his head as he slipped the brushes, bristles pointing up, into a jar beside others just like it inside the cabinet. "That she most certainly was," he said heavily, procuring a piece of pristine, white paper. He paused, turning to look over his shoulder and stopping just short. "I must admit that I considered her somewhat of a mentor, though very few people ever knew that."

My heart squirmed in my chest. Was it entirely possible that I had completely misread the look Mrs. Milbourn had given him that night?

"She taught me everything I know," he said, gesturing around to all the paintings, those finished and those that were works in progress. "Well, perhaps not *everything,* but she inspired me from a young age."

I looked around and it struck me that there were similarities. He seemed to use the same sorts of colors that she did, the same gentle hand when applying them that I had noticed in the piece hanging in Catherine's hall. I could see a similarity, an origin of inspiration.

"My father used to take me to see her exhibits whenever they would open," he said, bringing the paper to a table beside me, smoothing it out with his long, narrow fingers. A small half smile stretched over his face. "My favorite happened to be when I had just turned ten. You see, I always wished to be an artist, but my father had frowned on it, saying that I had to take over the family canning company. My brother and I both. My brother wished to pursue that path, and I...did not. I went to see her exhibit, and I still remember it like it was yesterday."

He returned to the cabinet, pulling down a narrow box of charcoal, carrying it back to the table where I stood.

"It was called *The Light*, and I was astounded by her paintings. She captured light in a way I had never seen, in several mediums; watercolor, acrylic, oil – " He held up the small box. "Even charcoal. That was the day I decided I wanted to be a painter, just as she primarily was."

"That's a very touching story..." I said.

He gave me a tight smile. "Yes, I suppose it is." He pulled up a stool and sat down upon it. "She told me that day that she could see the same fire in my eyes that she had, a real passion and gift for art. She then agreed to help give me some training, and as such..." He gestured around. "Because of a few simple lessons and some encouragement, here I am today."

"That's remarkable," I said, now feeling slightly guilty.

He looked at the paper spread out across the table. "They have asked me to speak at her funeral in two days, and I have yet to decide if I should."

It surprised me that he was so forthright about his relationship with her.

He looked up and smiled, his face brightening. "I'm terribly sorry. I don't quite know why I have been telling you all this." His gaze warmed. "I suppose you are just the trustworthy sort, aren't you?"

My face colored, and I didn't know what to say.

"Now, this is something I do with every client," he said. "I should like to do a preliminary sketch of you. It shouldn't take any longer than ten or fifteen minutes. Then we can schedule a time either for you to come back here to sit for the painted portrait, or I could come to your home and work there, say...once a week?"

"I think your father would be pleased with the latter arrangement," Miles suggested suddenly, surprising me by striding over. "He would be most interested in meeting Mr. Steeles."

The artist arched a brow as he surveyed Miles. "British, hmm? What brings you over to this side of the world?"

"A grand adventure," Miles said flatly.

Mr. Steeles smiled easily at me. "I see. Very well, no need to upset any fathers. I shall just have you write your address here, and we can get started."

The sketch took only ten minutes, just as he said, and then Miles and I were on our way. Mr. Steeles gave me the sketch he had done up of me, and I found myself unable to stop looking at it as we started the car ride back toward the house.

Miles turned around at the first stop sign, regarding me with question.

I looked up from the paper, from the long, gentle lines of charcoal that made up what Mr. Steeles saw in me.

"It's a good likeness," he said, his finger pointing to the sheet I laid across the seat beside me. "Though I think he made your eyes too narrow."

I glanced at the sheet. I thought he did well with my eyes...perhaps even making me look a little prettier than I truly was.

"I imagine his painting will be adequate, but I have a hard time believing he will be able to capture the real you on such slight acquaintance," Miles said.

"I don't suppose an artist requires much acquaintance to paint a portrait. He is a professional, after all," I pointed out.

"Perhaps. But it struck me back there that his interest in you was rather beyond the professional. I am sorry if it is not my place to say so. I simply think you should be aware."

"Your warning is noted," I said. "However, I really see no cause for concern."

"Then forgive me if I suggest one," Miles said. "I must tell you, Miss Sylvia, I had wondered about your true intention for visiting him, at first. I say *had* wondered because your purpose became clear quickly." He turned the wheel hard to the left as he made a wide turn down a side street. "And if it is obvious to me, there is a risk it was to him as well."

I looked away, reluctant either to deny or confirm his suspicion.

"I suspected you might want to look into the death of that woman from the gallery. He was surprisingly talkative and told you more than I am certain you expected. But you shouldn't allow that to make you overconfident."

"It seems that I have no idea what I am doing," I said, suddenly discouraged. "I have no idea why I felt the need to go and talk to him. I don't even know what I expected to find..." I sighed.

"You needed to learn the truth about what really happened," he said in a quiet voice. "I suppose I can understand that. It's commendable, if not a bit foolish."

My brow furrowed. "You have quite the cheek today, speaking as freely as you have been."

"My apologies," he said. "I never meant to upset you. I am simply observing, and it is my job to look after your family's interests however I can."

"Yes, well..." I said. I hesitated, the next question burning inside me. "What did you think about what he said?"

"What did you think first?" he asked. "What was your initial assessment?"

"Well, I believe I might have misjudged him," I said. "Hearing the way he spoke of Mrs. Milbourn made me think the look I saw between the pair of them was innocent enough. I thought there was anger, but perhaps it was more akin to disappointment."

"And then?" Miles asked.

"I don't know," I said. "Maybe hearing his side of it changed my mind. It was clear how much he admired her. It is no small claim to say she was a mentor of sorts to him."

"That's true," Miles said. "Were you suspicious that he might have been the one to kill her?"

"It was the first possibility I had to work with," I said. "It seems I was wrong, though."

"Perhaps, but do not forget..." he said. "It is often those closest to the victims that have reason for killing them. I understand your desire to know the truth and to accurately discern how people are acting and thinking, but that doesn't mean your initial instincts were unfounded."

"I suppose..." I said. "It's difficult to be sure."

"So...what do you plan to do now?" he asked.

"I don't rightly know," I said. "Perhaps when he comes to do the portrait, I will question him more. Maybe I could..." I stopped, shaking my head. "Perhaps I shouldn't. Maybe I should abandon this whole notion all together."

Miles didn't agree or disagree, and simply continued to drive.

We arrived at home, Miles letting me in through the front door.

"Miss Sylvia?" he murmured as I walked passed him.

I stopped, looking at him.

"If you do decide to pursue this...I hope you will be careful."

I stared at him. "Of course, I never intended to be anything else," I said. "But...thank you."

6

"You cannot be serious!"

Joan did not at all take kindly to my answer as to why I had left in such a hurry that morning. Feeling she would probably discover the truth if I tried to withhold it, I had confessed my errand to her when she asked me about it over lunch. Conveniently, our parents had already left the table by then.

I said nothing now, staring down instead at the pudding that our cook Gibbins had made for us all, as a special token of his appreciation to Father and Mother to mark his tenth anniversary of working for our family. Boasting hints of lemon, sweet and silky, with comforting notes of vanilla, it lifted my spirits after my encounter with Mr. Steeles.

"Why do you feel the need to get yourself involved

in this?" Joan asked. "You *do* realize it isn't necessary, don't you?"

"Of course I know that," I said. "If it helps you to feel any better, I learned nothing."

"Does this mean you are still going to follow through with other options?" she asked, her eyes narrowing. "Nosing around the city until you find someone who might have had reason enough to harm that woman?"

"I don't know," I admitted.

Joan scoffed, crossing her arms. "The answer is quite simple, Sylvia. You should *not* get your hands dirty again. What are you going to do if Mr. Adams learns you are sticking your nose into such a gruesome thing?"

I looked up at her, surprised to realize I had nearly forgotten about Fredrick Adams. But there was no knowing if I would ever see him again, so I saw no reason to worry about what he would think of me now. "I never said to what extent I might look into the death –"

"The extent should be none," Joan said.

She glared over her shoulder at Miles who had joined us for the meal, at least in the sense of being present in the room. He had found a set of Mother's silver to polish, most of which sparkled as if it were new, in a neat row along the buffet. It struck me that it was an odd chore to be carrying out in front of us, rather than back in the kitchen, and I wondered if he only did it as an excuse to be close enough to eavesdrop on our conversation.

"And you!" Joan snapped at him. "You took her there!"

Miles turned to look at her, and nodded. "That I did, Miss. Just as Mr. Shipman would have wished. It seemed unlikely he would want her to go alone."

Her eyes narrowed. "If you are half as perceptive as you make yourself out to be, then surely you should have realized why my sister wanted to visit Steeles. She has never wanted a commissioned piece for herself in all the time I have known her. Now an artist dies at an event we attended, and the very next day she happens to visit someone associated with the dead woman?"

"I appreciate your thinking so highly of me, Miss," Miles said with only a hint of irony, giving a spot on the side of a pitcher a fervent scrub with his linen cloth. "Naturally, I realized rather quickly what Miss Sylvia wanted when she began to speak with the man. In truth, I can see why she might have suspected him, given how you had both witnessed what you did the night before."

"We witnessed nothing," Joan said.

"I think your sister would beg to differ," Miles said.

They both turned to look at me, and I shrugged uncomfortably. "I may have misread the look between them. It was obvious there was *something* to it, but maybe it was not as hostile as I first suspected."

Joan groaned, leaning back in her chair. "What makes you think you will be able to find anything the police didn't?" she asked.

I hesitated for a moment. "I did discover the truth about Uncle Walter's death," I said. "Well before the police might have, if they even had the time, given the state of things right now."

"And so you think you can take on any murder that happens to cross your path?" she asked.

"I don't imagine there will be more," I said. "At least, I would hope not."

"That isn't the point," Joan said. "This isn't your problem! Why do you feel the need to intrude?"

"Because we were the last to speak with her alive," I said. "It could have been anyone, but it was us. That gives us a duty to the dead. And besides, remember how difficult it was for our family when Uncle Walter was killed? Wouldn't it be worthwhile to give this woman's family the same sort of closure we needed?"

Joan shook her head. "You are unbelievable," she said. "It's as if I hardly know you anymore."

She leapt from her chair and stomped out of the room, not bothering to catch the heavy dining room door on her way out, letting it slam shut.

I stared at the door, uncertain what to do.

"She'll be all right," Miles said, breaking the tense silence.

"We have our share of quarrels, but she doesn't usually get this angry with me..." I said.

"She's only looking out for you," he said, carrying the last of the polished silver back to the glass-fronted cabinet where it was typically stored. "She is probably just worried you're in danger."

"Perhaps she is right," I said. "It would not be entirely wrong for me to leave this in the hands of someone far more capable."

"True," Miles said, closing the cabinet doors. "Though there is no telling how much effort the proper authorities will put into the matter, or whether they will ever arrive at a satisfactory conclusion. They have been known to make mistakes."

His thinking followed my own a little too closely. There was also an uncomfortable truth nudging at the back on my mind, one I had no intention of admitting aloud. Maybe it wasn't only justice I was chasing. Maybe it was satisfaction for my own curiosity. I wanted to know the truth about what had happened to Mrs. Milbourn, and maybe I felt it would be personally satisfying to be the one to uncover it.

I pursed my lips, shoving the thought aside. "I suppose I don't rightly know what to do next," I said. "I don't even know where to begin."

"Well..." he said, slipping into the seat beside me at

the dining table. He dropped his voice, glancing briefly at the door. "If you would so desire, I might reach out to some of my acquaintances and see what I can learn about the woman who died."

I blinked at him. "Why would you do that?"

"This matter seems to be important to you, and whatever my friends find might help give you some direction, a place to start, as Mr. Steeles is still questionable."

"Right..." I said. "Best not to pin all my suspicions on one person."

"Though I am not yet willing to dismiss him entirely," Miles said.

"He didn't seem the sort," I said. "After meeting him, I have to agree with Catherine Waters' assessment of him as irritating but harmless. Still, I agree that it's too early to be confident about that."

Miles nodded. "For the time being, I will send a message to a few people who would likely have connections to the art community. Might you spell the victim's name for me?"

"Of course," I said. I gave him what he wanted to know, and he bid me farewell, leaving the dining room.

My enthusiasm sank, after he was gone.

Am I a fool to pursue this matter further? Miles seems to approve, but it's hardly a decision for my butler to make. And as for making use of Miles' connections, how can I forget so quickly the secret I learned about his past? Why do

I continue to act as if he is reliable, as if there is some innocent explanation for that newspaper article about him, when I have no reason to believe him trustworthy, aside from my own instincts?

The door to the dining room opened, Miles peering back inside. "Miss Sylvia, there is someone here to see you."

I stood right to my feet. "Who is it?" I asked.

"A man named Mr. Adams?" he asked, his brow furrowing. "He said that he knew you were not expecting him, and as such if you needed him to come back at a better time, he would."

That was certainly tempting. I wasn't at all prepared to meet with him. In fact, I was surprised he had taken the time to look me up. But when I thought of sending him away, I could immediately hear the voices of my mother, father, and Joan all at once asking with incredulity as to why I hadn't at least given him a moment of my time. Mr. Adams was known and respected around town, after all. I especially wouldn't hear the end of it from Joan.

"That's all right," I said, coming around the table. "I shall meet him, if he has bothered to come all this way to speak with me."

Miles smiled politely, but I noticed the usual genial glint in his gaze wasn't there. "Right this way, then," he said.

He walked with me to the door, hanging back as we reached the foyer.

Mr. Adams stood near the door, his hat in hand as he surveyed my father's antique tapestry hanging just inside the doorway.

"Miss Sylvia," he said, noticing as I approached. He grinned. "How pleased I am that you were able to see me."

"Thank you for coming all the way here," I said.

He glanced back at the tapestry. "I was simply admiring this lovely piece," he said. "Is it Turkish?"

"It is indeed," I said. "A gift from my uncle...my late uncle."

His smile faltered. "I'm terribly sorry," he said.

"It isn't your fault," I said. "How can I help you, Mr. Adams?"

He spun the hat in his hands like a wheel, hand over hand. Was he nervous? Really? Someone as handsome and polished as he was? "I was in the neighborhood when I realized I was very close to your home. I hope you'll forgive me, but I sought out one of our mutual friends for your address."

My cheeks flushed pink. "Catherine Waters, I presume?" I asked.

His smile returned. "Indeed. She said you would likely be home during the day, and so, I thought I might make my request in person instead of through a note or telephone call."

"A request?" I asked. "What sort of request?"

He opened his mouth, but his eyes darted over my shoulder.

"I thought I heard someone at the door," said Joan from the stairwell. She strolled over, smirking back and forth between Mr. Adams and I. "And what a surprise it is! Mr. Adams, how good it is to see you again so soon."

He let out a small laugh. "The joy is mine, Miss Joan."

She waved a dismissive hand. "You must call us Joan and Sylvia. It is not as if this is our first meeting. Have you come to see my sister? Oh, how wonderful."

He laughed again. "That I did," he said. He turned back to me. "I had hoped you might join me for dinner at my home this coming Friday...Sylvia."

"For dinner?" I asked, the color in my face deepening. Already?

"Your sister would be invited, of course," he said, hurriedly. "I am having a few of my friends over as well. Unfortunately, Catherine Waters has informed me she is unable to attend, but said I should still go through with asking you."

"We would absolutely *love* to," Joan said. "Isn't this just marvelous, Sylvia?"

I looked at her, and noticed a flash in her eyes, a tightness to her broad smile that spoke far louder of warning than praise. I couldn't argue with her, not in front of Mr. Adams. She had put me in a position where I couldn't refuse him without appearing horrendously rude.

Joan, why are you doing this to me? I thought.

So I smiled up at Mr. Adams. "We would be pleased to join you," I said.

"Wonderful," he said, clapping his hands together, a relieved sounding chuckle escaping his lips. "I shall leave my address with your butler then, shall I? Dinner will be served at eight, but everyone always gathers for conversation and games around five...if you would wish to join us for that, of course."

"We would love to," Joan said brightly.

"We look forward to it," I said, perhaps a bit less enthusiastically than she.

"I am pleased to hear it," he said. "Now then, I must be on my way. I don't wish to keep either of you from anything important. Thank you for allowing me a few moments of your time."

"We were happy to do so," Joan said.

Miles appeared with a pen and paper ready in hand, allowing Mr. Adams to leave his address.

"Farewell, ladies. Enjoy the day!" he said, and with that, he was off.

Miles closed the door behind him, but not before Joan rounded on me. "You were going to refuse him, weren't you?"

"I – " I began, but she didn't give me a chance.

"Sylvia, are you mad?" she asked. "He seems to be a catch. Attractive, charming, well connected. He's obviously very keen on you, and yet you seem far too distracted to give him your attention."

I frowned. "It's all happening so quickly. We hardly know the man. I might have wanted some time to consider – "

"Consider what?" she asked. "Snubbing someone like Fredrick Adams? Is that really a wise choice?"

"I never said I wanted to snub him," I said.

Her eyes narrowed. "I might have guessed at the gallery the other night," she said. "You were ready to hand him over to me if I so much as showed the slightest interest. You didn't want to have anything to do with him in the first place, did you?"

"Why are you pushing him at me so hard?" I asked, genuinely confused.

"Because I think it's high time you involved yourself in something less gruesome than murder," she said. "And Mr. Adams is a suitable candidate to be that something. Father and Mother could hardly complain. He's entirely respectable. I just think his acquaintance is worth exploring further."

"I suppose there *is* something pleasant about him," I admitted reluctantly. "He's certainly not bad looking..."

"Then why don't you want to give him a chance?"

she pressed. "What is it that's consuming your thoughts so much you would consider ignoring him? And don't say this is about Mrs. Milbourn's death, because we've already decided you are going to stay away from that."

"*You* decided," I corrected her.

She ignored that. "Or is there someone else you're secretly interested in?" she continued.

For some reason, Miles' face passed through my mind. Miles, who was all together more interesting than Mr. Adams, more handsome and capable, more mysterious – I shook my head. "No, it's no one, it's nothing."

Joan's glare told me that she didn't believe me. "This dinner will be good for you, then," she snapped. "It will give you the chance to get out of the house, and distract you from whatever it is you can't seem to get out of your mind."

"That's perfectly fine," I said. "I never said I didn't want to go. It just surprised me, is all."

She relaxed ever so slightly. "Why?" she asked. "When he made his interest perfectly obvious the first time me met?"

I shrugged, keenly aware that Miles stood nearby, straightening a family portrait that hung near the stairwell.

"All I want is for you to give him a chance," Joan said.

"And if I do that, but ultimately decide he's not for me?" I asked. "Will you respect my wishes?"

"Yes," she said. "Of course."

"I hope you remember your words," I said. "I don't want to have to remind you of this conversation later."

"I won't forget," she said, but I could see some reservation in her eyes.

"Very well," I said. "I suppose a quiet, cheerful evening wouldn't do me any harm."

7

"Stop tugging at your hair," Joan scolded me as we stood outside Mr. Adams' exquisite manor home on the northern side of Long Island.

"You shouldn't have arranged it so tightly..." I grumbled, nonetheless lowering my hand. She had pinned my short locks up in such a way that the pins dug into my scalp at the nape of my neck, and I could hardly stand it every time I turned my head. She assured me that it looked as she had hoped, and warned me not to touch it.

She glared at me again, hard, as we waited for the door to be answered.

To our surprise, it was only a few moments later, and we were greeted by Mr. Adams himself.

"If it isn't the Shipman sisters," he said, beaming at

us. “I’m so glad you could make it.” He looked out after us, staring up at the sky overhead. “Seems you missed the weather, too.”

“It snowed until we reached the bridge to the island,” Joan said. She smiled. “Don’t you just love the first few snowfalls of the winter?”

“I’m sorry to disappoint you, but I cannot say that I do,” Mr. Adams said with a shy grin. “Winter is nearly intolerable, in my opinion.”

I perked up.

He glanced at me. “It seems I have struck a chord, Sylvia.”

“You have,” I said. “I also am not pleased with the cold.”

His smile deepened. “I am pleased to hear that we already have so much in common. But where are my manners? Please come in, we can continue our jovial bantering in the warmth of the house.”

Joan hopped over the threshold at his gesturing, and just as I stepped out to follow her, I glanced over my shoulder.

Miles stood near the car, bundled up in a thick, wool coat and leather gloves. The scarf tied around his neck only brought out the rich green of his eyes, as similar as they were in color. He gave me a small nod, as I looked.

He had assured us that he would wait outside for us to leave, as there was little sense in driving all the way back to Sutton Place to wait until ten or eleven, especially if the weather was going to get worse. "*I won't leave you both stranded out here,*" he had said. "*I do not believe your father would approve.*"

There seemed to be a great deal that he thought our father would not *approve* of as of late.

"There we are," Mr. Adams said as his butler hiding behind the door closed it for us.

Immediately, warmth enveloped and comforted me. Shedding my heavy fur coat, which the butler appeared at my side to take, I turned to look around.

The inside of the home seemed to reflect the outside, with the same tall ceilings supported by pillars very much like the four columns out in front. Large windows behind us washed the room in light, which reached all the way to the bottom of twin staircases running up either side of the room. They met in the middle, rising over our heads, and disappeared onto the next floor.

Our footsteps echoed on the black and white tile floor as our host led us down the hall passing beneath the meeting point of the stairs.

"Your home is...magnificent," Joan said, gaping at the sheer size of it. Our house had the top of the line luxuries, but his manor held something ours in the city simply could not; space.

"I am glad you think so," he said with a grin over

his shoulder. "I realize it is much quieter than city life, but it has its charms."

I felt a stirring of worry. *If this is his home and not the home of his parents...then this is where his future wife will live, if he ever marries.* I chewed on my lower lip as he told Joan about the beautiful sitting room we passed through. *Perhaps I am getting ahead of myself, but if his interest in me continues...*

It was not lost on me that this could be *my* house if I played my cards right.

Strangely, the thought of living in this immense, echoing house didn't appeal to me a great deal.

"Sylvia?"

I looked up to see both Mr. Adams and Joan looking at me, the latter far more incredulous than the first. "Yes?" I asked.

Mr. Adams smiled. "I asked if you would care for some coffee?"

"Oh, yes, please," I said. "I was just looking around your lovely home. I suppose I got a bit distracted."

"It's quite all right," he said with a chuckle. "I'm certain you will like this room, then, if you have been impressed thus far."

He stepped into a room at the end of the hall, where both wooden doors had been thrown open... and my jaw dropped.

We stood at the mouth of a ballroom, but unlike any I had seen. The far wall was rounded, and filled with windows out to the gorgeous property, which must have been lush and green in the spring time.

An enormous chandelier, consisting of sparkling crystals tied together in long rows all brought together at the center and pinned to the ceiling, hung in the middle of the room. It reminded me of a glittering cushion, the way it draped and shone. With every step I took, those tiny crystals overheard shimmered like the surface of a sunny lake.

A long table with enough chairs to seat at least three dozen people sat beneath it. Candelabras of polished silver stood all along it, atop a crimson tablecloth.

Six other guests were at one end of the table, where generous numbers of plates and bowls were waiting, all laden with food and drink. The guests already there laughed and carried on with one another.

My heart sank as I didn't recognize a single one of them.

"It is never a comforting thing to leave the room and return to find all one's guests laughing," Mr. Adams said, approaching the table with a chortle.

The young man nearest him, red-headed and strikingly handsome, barked a laugh. "Fredrick, you must hear the way Elizabeth tells this story," he said, grabbing hold of Mr. Adams' arm. "It really is quite funny."

"All right, but allow me to introduce my guests

first," Mr. Adams said. "I know you'll all be on your *best behavior,* yes?" he asked.

The others smirked or nodded as Joan and I came to stand beside him at the head of the table.

"Some of you might know Joan Shipman," he began, gesturing to her. "And this is her sister, Sylvia."

"Joan?" asked a woman with a long neck and pouting lips. "Did you perform at Central Park last summer?"

Joan beamed. "I did. Yes," she said.

The woman grinned. "I thought I recognized you. You played that servant girl, didn't you?"

Joan nodded. "That was me, yes. How nice to be recognized."

"Is this the woman you were telling us about?" asked the handsome red-headed man.

"That she is," Mr. Adams said, smiling down at me. "Now, ladies, please go ahead and take your seats. Dinner will be arriving momentarily and I think you will be most pleased by it."

Joan took my hand and steered me down the table. She squeezed so hard I began to feel my own heartbeat in my fingers. It struck me that, despite my sister's easy manner, we were both feeling equally out of place. She was simply better at hiding it than I.

"Now, go on then, let's hear the story," Mr. Adams said with a sweeping gesture, taking his seat at the end of the table.

The woman who had spoken to Joan, named Elizabeth, it seemed, clapped her hands together. "All right," she said with a grin. "You must understand how Mrs. Rand is most of the time. She is pretentious at the best of times. Well, she strode into my father's garden party, during the last nice day before the winter turned, acting as if she was the most honored guest. She wasted no time telling my mother and I precisely how her trip to Italy had been, how she had not noticed a thing about the decline – well, didn't my mother tell her it would be insensitive to speak so freely of her wealth, given the hardships some were facing – not us, of course, but she was trying to be kind – and would you believe that she laughed at my mother?"

The woman beside her gasped. "She did not!"

"She did," said Elizabeth. "And not only that, but she told my mother off for even suggesting she would be so tactless. We all knew she would be, *she* knew she would be...well, I was not going to sit and allow her to treat my mother that way. I looked her straight in the eye and told her I knew she was lying. She could only stare at me, and asked what she could possibly be lying about, and that's when I told her I knew full well that some of her husband's money was in real estate, and many of the places in the Upper East Side have recently gone up for sale."

"You think he is selling them?" asked the first man.

"Oh, for *certain,*" Elizabeth said. "It was very clear, just by the look on her face."

The other woman laughed behind her hands. "Oh, that would be confirmation enough!" she said. "She had to have been stunned speechless!"

"Yes, she was," Elizabeth said. "She could say nothing to the contrary. All she could do was walk away."

The rest of the guests burst out laughing, and Joan and I simply looked at one another.

We knew Mrs. Rand. A good friend of our mother, she frequented our home on a regular basis. We had heard of the hardship her family had endured recently. They had indeed had to sell many of their properties, as many of the occupants could no longer afford them.

"It seems there are many ladies of high society who have lost all good sense," Mr. Adams said from the head of the table, still smirking. "When was the last time any of you spoke with Mrs. Leavens?"

No one answered.

"Louise Leavens? It's been months, I believe," Elizabeth said. "Why?"

"I've heard that she has been kicked off the board at the gallery," he said.

My ears pricked up. *Surely he isn't talking about –*

"Which gallery?" his handsome friend asked.

"The one next to Central Park," he said with a

wave. "I can never remember the name. I was there recently for the *Sea of Glass* exhibit for Mr. Gardener."

It is the same gallery! I thought, my stomach dropping.

His eyes shifted to me, as if my thoughts had summoned his attention. "I heard of this from our mutual friend Catherine Waters," he told me.

"Why is this significant?" asked Elizabeth.

"Well, it seems Mrs. Leavens didn't take too *kindly* to being asked to resign," Mr. Adams said. "According to Miss Waters, she heard from her father – the owner of the gallery, mind you – that Mrs. Leavens made a real show about it."

"How so?" asked another man at the end of the table, his dark hair hanging somewhat in his eyes, his expression slack and disinterested.

"Apparently, she publicly threatened to ruin the exhibition, particularly the *Sea of Glass* exhibit," he said. "It was meant to be their most successful showing of the year, given Mr. Gardener's involvement. I suppose it doesn't surprise me to think she would want to disrupt it. She likely helped plan it."

I straightened, glancing sidelong at Joan. She, too, stared at him, eyes narrowing and brow furrowing. Without a word, I knew she was thinking the same thing I was.

"Wasn't the exhibit last week?" asked Elizabeth. "I

was out of town, naturally, visiting family in Philadelphia."

"Yes, apparently this all happened before it," Mr. Adams said.

"But wait – " said the handsome redhead. "Wasn't there some sort of...attack that happened that very night?"

Mr. Adams nodded again, a smile brimming on his face. Clearly, his friend was making his point for him.

"Now that you mention it, I do recall hearing something from my mother about Mrs. Leavens recently," said the woman to Elizabeth's left. She tapped her chin with the point of her finger, her gaze turned upward. "She made some sort of wild rant...was that the same incident?"

"It very well may have been," Mr. Adams said.

"I have never heard of Mrs. Leavens acting out in such a way," said the dark haired man, voicing a question of my own. He looked at Mr. Adams as if he had somehow affronted him. "How certain are you of this?"

"Without a doubt," Mr. Adams said. "I heard it straight from Miss Waters." His head turned toward Joan. "She is your friend too. Have you heard of this?"

Joan's cheeks flushed, and she folded her arms. "More my sister's friend, but no, I haven't heard of this," she said, lifting her chin.

"So, this woman completely takes leave of her good sense, flies off on a rampage against the board, threatening to ruin it...and then a woman is attacked and killed, right in the middle of it all?" asked Elizabeth with a gasp. Then her face split into a smile as she let out a sharp, shrill laugh. "What in the world happened between the pair of them?"

She is taking genuine pleasure in all this, I thought.

"Perhaps Mr. Leavens came on to Mrs. Milbourn," laughed the redhead, leaning back in his chair to hold his belly as he chuckled. "That would certainly sour the pair of them."

"But how would she have managed to get a knife in her back without anyone seeing?" asked the dark-haired man beside him, looking as displeased as I felt.

"How do you know Mrs. Leavens didn't have it in her handbag?" asked the other woman, twirling a thick curl of ebony hair around her finger. "*Oh, pardon me, Mrs. Milbourn. I only wanted to stop and tell you how pleased I am to have worked with you all these years –* stab!"

A peel of laughter came from the guests at the far end of the table, as Joan, the other young man, and I, all sat silent and uncomfortable.

One lady spoke up. "Maybe it was sheer jealousy. Everyone was jealous of Mrs. Milbourn. Her success, her fame, her enormous fortune. They were about the same age, weren't they? They must have worked together a great deal. Maybe they were old friends, and had some sort of terrible fight." She giggled. "*No, I will* not *give you the name of my seamstress! You will have to find your own!"*

More laughter filled the room, bouncing off the walls in the large space...but it felt hollow to me.

"What more likely happened is that Mrs. Milbourn had some sort of say in who was on the board," Mr. Adams said. "As well respected as she was, she might have had sway, even if she didn't sit on the board officially."

"Ooh," said Elizabeth, her eyes growing wide. "The plot thickens!"

They all shared another laugh.

"Well...we have no idea what happened," Mr. Adams said. "Nor do the police, it seems. I imagine we would have heard one way or the other by now."

"Not surprising," said the redhead. "They never get anything done, do they?"

The conversation turned to other things then, but I could no longer concentrate on it.

I glanced at Joan, my stomach in knots. I didn't want to look down the table any more. If anything, I felt somewhat alien in this place now.

I gestured to Joan and stood to my feet.

"I'm sorry, Mr. Adams, but I'm suddenly not feeling all too well," I said stiffly.

"Oh, don't be sick on me!" cried Elizabeth, leaning away from me, her nose wrinkling.

"Yes, of – of course," our host said, sliding his own

chair out. He came around to offer me his arm, and guided Joan and I to the door.

"Thank you for the party, Mr. Adams," I said, unable to take the silence much longer. "I had a lovely time."

"You're very welcome," he said, in a tone equally as heavy as the one I had used.

He opened the front door, and my eyes fell upon Miles standing beside the car, precisely where we had left him. His eyes widened when he saw Joan and I returning so quickly, and he hurried up the steps to meet us. "Is everything all right?" he asked, his words like puffs of smoke hanging in the air.

"Apparently Miss Sylvia has taken ill," Mr. Adams said, walking past him, and laying his hand over my own still in the crook of his arm. "You must get her home at once."

"Certainly, sir," Miles said, pulling open the car door.

Joan slid in first, and Mr. Adams helped me inside. Before closing the door, he gave me a small smile. "I am sorry, you know. I was hoping we could have spent more time together."

I tried to return his smile, but all I could think about was the laughter now ringing in my head. "Perhaps another time," I said.

"I would like that," he said, and closed the door.

Miles slid into the front seat and started the engine. Without a word, he accelerated down the drive.

"Well, that was quite a little scene you played," Joan said as Miles drove us through the large gates at the mouth of the drive. "Perhaps you are a better actress than I."

"What do you mean?" I asked, surprised at her sarcasm.

She rolled her eyes. "You're not ill," she said, but then her face softened. "...Though I suppose I cannot blame you for not wishing to sit through another *second* of that ridiculous conversation."

I nodded. "I didn't care for the callous way they were speaking of Mrs. Milbourn, as if her death was all a joke. As if she wasn't a real person."

Joan shrugged. "Just because they behaved as if they felt no sympathy doesn't mean they truly don't," she said.

"What do you mean?" I asked.

"Just that," she said. "It is the way of artists. They are the same as those in my circles. They pretend, so no one really knows what they are feeling. Those people might have all been acting, for all you know."

"That doesn't make it any better," I said.

"No, maybe it doesn't," Joan said. "But that's only part of what's on your mind."

"True." I frowned. "They think that woman they

spoke of, Mrs. Leavens, might have had something to do with Mrs. Milbourn's death," I said.

"And for some reason, you want to look into this Mrs. Leavens now," Joan said.

"I never said that," I said.

"Your face told the story for you," Joan snapped. "Why are you so intent on involving yourself in the first place?"

I remained quiet for a moment. I noticed Miles glance at me in the rearview mirror.

"There is something vastly different about wanting justice for her...and making little of her death by joking about it," I said.

Joan said nothing.

"Those people back there will do nothing to help," I said. "That much is clear. They only see her murder as an amusing story to share at the dinner table."

"I will give you that," Joan said flatly.

"But they inadvertently did something useful," I said. "They gave me a name that I can pursue. I'm taking that as a sign that I am *meant* to look into it."

Joan studied my face. "You really believe you can get to the bottom of all this, don't you?" she asked.

"I don't rightly know what I believe anymore," I said. "I wanted to be done with it, but it seems that it doesn't want to be done with me."

Joan huffed, rolling her eyes. "Fine. *Fine.* If you are so determined, then..." She deflated a bit, sighing. "...

Then might I ask you not to do anything that will bring embarrassment to our family? I think Father has enough on his mind these days."

"Of course," I said. "I intend to be as discreet in my inquiries as I can be."

"Good," she said, then her head turned to Miles, who seemed to be very interested in being as quiet as possible. "And you will do what you can to keep her out of trouble, Miles. I am counting on you."

He turned around and gave my sister a wink. "You can trust me, Miss Joan," he said. "As can you, Miss Sylvia."

"Thank you, Miles," I said in as neutral a tone as possible, before turning to stare out the window.

As we drove on toward home, we all descended into silence, each of us lost in our own thoughts.

I hope you know what you're doing, a small voice in the back of my head said. *And I hope you realize the deep water you're wading into...both with Mrs. Milbourn...and Miles.*

8

"You're thinking about going to visit her today, aren't you?"

The question came seemingly out of nowhere. Snow had come in the night, not long after Joan and I had arrived home from Mr. Adams', burying the sidewalk out in front of the house. It nestled in the windows and clung to the branches of the trees lining the street as if trying to form a perfect mold of them.

Father, unable to go out to his office, decided to remain at home at our mother's request. He had barely been seen, still taking the opportunity to work as many hours as he would have had he left that morning as intended, but Mother seemed content to know at least he was under the same roof as the rest of us. Her own plans hadn't changed, as it seemed to be one of the rare days where she hadn't made plans with any of her friends.

On such a cool, quiet day, she had wanted to take advantage of it fully with both Joan and I in residence. She planned for games, for times of reading, for Joan to practice a monologue she had been working on... but instead had settled beside the fire in the parlor and fallen promptly asleep after lunch.

I looked up from the violin that lay across my lap; I had taken the chance to busy myself with polishing it. I hadn't had the strength to touch it since our uncle's passing; even now it was sad to see it, to pluck its strings and know that he and I wouldn't play together again.

"Who do you mean?" I asked, my eyes finally meeting Joan's.

She frowned at me, letting the book in her hands fall against her lap. "You know perfectly well who I mean," she said. She eyed Mother, dropping her voice. "You mean to go and speak with Mrs. Leavens, don't you?"

I also eyed Mother, whose head had lolled some time ago, resting now against the side of the winged chair, upholstered in her new favorite yellow poppies fabric. "To be honest, I haven't given it much thought."

Joan's eyebrow rose rather distinctly.

A small tremor of nerves passed down my spine. I knew Miles wasn't within earshot either, but that didn't mean I was terribly thrilled to be speaking about these matters. "I don't know," I finally admitted. "I know the timing of it all seems far too convenient – "

"That is my thought precisely," Joan said, surprising me. "To think Mrs. Leavens might have threatened all she did, only to see what happened? It might be coincidence, but it seems far too perfect, doesn't it?"

I lifted the violin off my lap and set it into its case on the sofa beside me, no longer feeling well enough to continue with such a usually pleasant task. "I take it you have been thinking about all this, too?"

She nodded. "It just seems so strange, doesn't it?" she asked. "What if she is the one who did it? What if Mrs. Milbourn said something about Mrs. Leavens being kicked off the committee? What if Mrs. Milbourn was the one who ensured that it happened?"

"That would certainly be reason enough for Mrs. Leavens to be angry," I said. "I will give you that."

"Well, then?" Joan asked. "Why don't you go and speak with her?"

"Are you asking me to?" I asked. "Seriously?"

"You are the one who seemed so determined to keep your nose squarely in this whole affair," Joan said. Then she shrugged. "And...I suppose I would like to see some justice for the poor woman, as well."

I stared at her. "That's quite a change of heart," I said.

"Yes, well, people change," she snapped. "That shouldn't be terribly shocking."

"You wanted me to bow out of this," I said. "You said it was foolish, would mar my reputation."

Joan, no longer looking at me, shrugged again. "Perhaps I was mistaken," she said. "If you resolve this, then you could find yourself some well deserved praise. It might even impress Mr. Adams. Not that it matters to you, does it?"

"What doesn't matter?" I asked.

Her eyes widened. "His opinion. You don't care one way or the other if he would be impressed. *That* isn't what matters to you."

I looked away. "I haven't made up my mind about him yet."

"Yes, you have," she said flatly. "And I believe you have little interest in him because you already have eyes for someone else." She quickly held up a hand as I started to protest. "I know you won't tell me who it is, and I've decided I'm all right with that for now. Whoever he is, he must be something to keep you as distracted as you are. Though I have to say, I'm having a hard time thinking who it could be..."

"There isn't anyone else," I said firmly, even as I tried desperately to keep my mind clear of all thoughts of anything...or anyone in particular.

"Suit yourself," she said with a shrug, getting to her feet. "It's obvious you haven't admitted it to yourself yet, and that's perfectly fine. You will eventually. But for now, I think you should go and do as you see fit. What we heard last night could be a good lead."

She strode to the door, pausing only to glance over her shoulder at me.

"Oh, and do be careful, won't you?" She grinned. "I will be all too happy to hear about it when you return home later." And then she was gone, leaving me alone with a gently snoring Mother.

Joan was right, much as I disliked admitting it. Even if the remarks about Mrs. Leavens were only made in jest, even if it might have been nothing more than idle gossip, did I really want to let this opportunity pass me by? What if no one else would take it seriously, even if it was the key to solving the tragedy of what happened that night at the gallery?

That might have been thinking a bit too highly of myself, imagining I was the only one who could discover the truth, but that didn't mean it couldn't be right.

I could take the information to the police and tell them what I have heard, I thought.

But even if they took me seriously, which they might not, wouldn't they want to know where I had heard all this? They would likely go and ask Mr. Adams. What would he think if he learned I had been the one to tip them off?

Joan may be right that I don't particularly care about

impressing him, but that certainly doesn't mean I wish to make trouble for him, I realized.

No, if I was going to take any of this information to the police, then I should first make sure of it myself. I would need an admission or perhaps a bit of evidence so the authorities could go straight to Mrs. Leavens, and not the source of the gossip.

I found Miles setting the table for dinner. "When you are finished with that, I would like you to drive me somewhere," I said.

He raised his eyebrows and glanced at me briefly, the warm light of the chandelier overhead highlighting his hair. "I would be happy to," he said, continuing to place the stemware at each of our place settings. "And where might I be taking you?"

I hesitated. I didn't actually know where Mrs. Leavens lived. He certainly wouldn't, either. "You'll have to ask Gibbins," I said. "I don't know the address."

Gibbons, as Miles must have been aware by now, was an unending source of knowledge in our home. Our cook tended to know a little of everyone in town's business, and if he had never heard of Mrs. Leavens, he would at least know how to learn where she lived.

"Very well," Miles said. "And what is the name I shall be telling him?"

"Mrs. Leavens," I said. "Louise is her first name, I believe."

Miles set down the last of the crystal glassware, and

bowed his head. "I shall be back shortly," he said, and disappeared through the swinging door to the kitchen.

I was relieved when he was gone. Why in the world was it so difficult to talk to him? Especially when it had once been so easy?

You know precisely why, I reprimanded myself. *He may very well not be the man you think he is.*

I didn't allow myself to dwell on that, however, as he returned just a few minutes later. "It seems this Mrs. Leavens has a reputation for changing her staff on a regular basis," he said, showing me a small piece of paper before pocketing it again. "Evidently, Gibbins' assistant Matthew used to work for her. He knew the address right off the top of his head."

"That's good news," I said. "Thank you for doing that."

"It's my pleasure," he said. "Well? Are you ready to go?"

We left at a reasonable time, which was good. At this hour, I would be more likely to catch Mrs. Leavens at home. I didn't quite know what to expect on the way, and was thankful that Miles gave me some space to think over my plan. The way he continued to glance over his shoulder at me told me he had heard all of my conversation with Joan on the ride back from Mr. Adams' dinner party. He must know full well the reason I was visiting Mrs. Leavens, but he asked no questions.

When we arrived, I worried that he would offer to go into the house with me.

He did not.

"I shall wait here for you," he said with a polite smile, standing back against the car.

I waited for some further comment, and when he gave none, I felt a small twinge of nervousness. *Is he avoiding me now?* I wondered.

I didn't have a great deal of time to consider the matter, uneasy as I was on approaching the front door. I had concocted a plan on my way here.

I knocked on the door.

A few things were working in my favor, one of which was that it was unlikely Mrs. Leavens would know me. She might recognize my name, though, and that was part of the plan I had come up with.

The door opened, and a face I had expected appeared. Not that I knew him but I knew by his uniform what his position in the house must be.

A broad grin spread across my face. "Good *afternoon*. Is Mrs. Leavens at home, by any chance?" The accent might have been a bit thick, but to my own ears it sounded believable enough.

It helped that I had practiced it more than a few times.

"Yes, she is," said the butler in a gruff tone. "Might I ask who is calling on her?"

I continued to smile. "My name is Miss Delilah

Meadows. She doesn't know me, so please let her know that."

Miss Delilah Meadows happened to be a character from a play Joan had been in last summer. Miss Meadows had been played by her friend and colleague Emma, but Joan had me read the lines over and over again, so much so that I had begun to learn the lines myself even as Joan learned hers. I hoped Mrs. Leavens hadn't heard of the play or the character, because if she did, then this entire endeavor would be ruined.

The butler nodded. "Please, come in out of the cold, Miss."

"Oh, thank you so much," I said, following him inside.

"I am surprised your chauffer was able to get the car out in this weather," he said, closing the door, preventing any more heat from escaping.

I rubbed my arms and smiled. "Yes, well, it was *most* important that I come and see Miss Leavens. Or is it Mrs. Leavens?"

"Mrs. Leavens, though her husband passed away two years ago," the butler answered. "Shall I leave you with your coat?"

"Yes, please," I said. "I'm afraid I'm not made for this weather. It's atrocious, isn't it?"

"Indeed it is," the butler said. "If you will wait here for a moment, I shall let Mrs. Leavens know you are here."

"Thank you," I said, and watched as he left me and disappeared around the corner.

Alone, I now had the chance to examine Mrs. Leavens' beautiful home. It reminded me a great deal of my own house, as it seemed that she and my mother shared an interest in bright fabrics and loud patterns; the bench beneath the window boasted brilliant red and pink roses, while the chair near the grandfather clock across the hall looked as if it might have been covered in real, tropical leaves. Drawing near proved that theory wrong, though the painted plants seemed very lifelike.

"Miss Meadows?"

I looked up at a woman descending the stairs – which were laid with a rather eye-tiring pattern of filigree and ferns of loud, coppery orange. She wore a dress of canary yellow, a matching feather pinned to her short, greying hair.

I forced a smile on my face even as a grimace twisted in my mind. *She has Mother's love of yellow, as well.* "Yes, that's me!" I said as cheerfully as I could manage. "And you are Mrs. Leavens, aren't you?"

"That I am," the woman said. "You must forgive me, but I do not recognize you or your name. Have we met before?"

She had come to stand before me, in the middle of the foyer. She smiled, folding her hands delicately in front of her.

"No, we haven't," I said, tossing some of my hair over my shoulder. "I had hoped to speak with Mrs. Leavens the artist. You are Mrs. Leavens, *the* artist, aren't you?"

This clearly pleased Mrs. Leavens. "Oh, well...yes, yes I am," she said. "Might I assume you are an admirer of my work?"

"I certainly am," I said, brightening. "But I am also an artist myself! Budding, of course, for I have been meeting a great many barriers in my path. I was told that you would be able to help me."

"Help you?" she asked, her smile fading somewhat. "Help you how?"

"By helping me to get one of my pieces into an exhibit!" I exclaimed. "I have been trying to get in touch with you for – for *weeks* now, but you have never been at home. Nor were you at the museum."

"The museum?" Mrs. Leavens asked, her face falling further. "You mean the gallery on the Upper East Side?"

"Yes, yes!" I said excitedly. "That is the one!" I frowned. "I went back and forth, checking here and there, but never could find you. Then I heard...I heard there had been a murder at the gallery."

I looked sheepishly up at Mrs. Leavens, and found a blank expression in reply.

For one horrifying moment, I wondered if she hadn't heard, hadn't known what had happened.

She seemed to return to life, however, and rather suddenly. She crossed her arms and looked away. I might have taken her for being disinterested in what I was saying, but the wrinkling of her nose told me otherwise. “Well, I am afraid you are too late to badger me about any of this,” she replied flatly. “I am no longer a part of the board. I cannot help you with anything you are asking of me.”

“Oh, but Mrs. Leavens, surely you still have connections there?” I asked, clasping my hands together, my eyes growing wide as I took an anxious step toward her. “Surely you must – ”

“You are mistaken,” she interrupted, her eyes flashing as she snapped at me. “If you want so desperately to be noticed, you had best go and bother someone who might have some control in the matter, someone who is still on the board.”

My heart began to race at her tone, which was so obviously bitter.

“Now, if you would be *so* kind as not to remind me of the unfortunate events that have happened to me of late, I shall ask you to be on your way.”

Worry that I was about to be back at the bottom of the search once again was enough to frustrate me, and that spilled easily over into the character I played. Perhaps it was nothing more than an excuse to let out the emotions that had been pent up within me, but I found myself bursting into dramatic tears right there in front of Mrs. Leavens.

In truth, I had started to sob into my hands with full control of myself, but then actual tears came flooding out, and it seemed that if I wanted it to be believable, then I certainly would convince her with real, puffy eyes and sniffling nose.

"Oh – Oh, come now, really," Mrs. Leavens scoffed. "Is this truly a matter worth crying over?"

I could hear a change of tone in her voice, and knew that if I just kept at it, perhaps she would be willing to listen to me...or perhaps reveal something to me in my supposedly fragile state. *It's working!* I thought.

"Well, I can't have you leaving the house in this state, can I?" Mrs. Leavens muttered, mostly to herself. "Come over here and have a seat." She guided me to a chair – the loud one with the lifelike leaves – and sat me down. "Pull yourself together, girl. If you have any hope of making it in the world of art, then you must grow a stiffer spine."

I did my best to comply, drying the surprisingly real tears from the corners of my eyes, hoping the hitch in my breathing would fade as the tears did.

A handkerchief appeared in my line of sight, and I looked up to see her offering it to me, though she appeared none too pleased.

"Thank – thank you," I said, taking it and dabbing

at my eyes. "You are very kind. I'm sorry to have – to have been so easily distressed."

Mrs. Leavens sighed, but said nothing further. I wondered if she had even heard me.

It seemed that she needed a bit more convincing. To aid me in my endeavor, I pulled some of the dialogue straight from the script, or at least as closely as I could remember it.

"I suppose...I suppose that my dreams are...that they are ruined!" I exclaimed, and buried my face in the handkerchief, pretending to cry once again. "What am I to do?"

"Oh, come now – "

"Now I shall never be able to show the world my art," I cried. "What does it matter if I am only met with a long hall of door after door that has been shut to me? There is no reason to continue, is there?"

That felt a bit forced, but my hold on the character was slipping.

"That's not true," Mrs. Leavens said. "Just because I cannot help you doesn't mean – "

"When I couldn't find you, I thought perhaps you had taken ill, or that you had been called away on some family trouble. Never would I have imagined someone as respected as you would have been – " I stopped, and looked up. "What *did* happen, Mrs. Leavens? Surely, it was the fault of someone else?"

Mrs. Leavens' face hardened, and she seemed

utterly lost as to what to do with me. "I am surprised you haven't heard about what a fool I made of myself..." she said. "I was asked to leave because I had begun to miss too many of the meetings. My...son, you see. He had taken ill. I had been traveling to visit him in the hospital in New Jersey, and so my responsibilities on the board were no longer being met."

My crying had stopped all together, and I stared up at her in surprise. When I had come here looking for an explanation, this was certainly not the one I thought I might find.

Her gaze, growing distant, fixed on a portrait on the wall. I hadn't noticed it when I had entered, my eye being drawn to the many patterns strewn around the space, but now that I looked, I saw a handsome family portrait done in a skillful hand.

"He is well now, but he will never be the same..." she said, her eyes narrowing as she studied the boy sitting on her knee in the portrait. He couldn't have been more than four or five years old at the time the painting had been done. "He lost the ability to walk for awhile and now needs the assistance of a cane – well, not that any of this matters to you."

I frowned. "I am very sorry to hear that," I said, dropping the pretense of Miss Meadows all together.

She shook her head. "It doesn't matter anymore. In my frustration, mingled with the little sleep I had been getting... Well, when they asked me to step down from the board, I had a momentary lapse in judgment and said some things – many things, really – that I never should have." She pursed her lips. "I embarrassed myself, creating a scene that will undoubtedly be on the tongue of every gossip that was present. I can tell you, it hasn't done my reputation in this city any good."

In the emotional state she describes, might she have gone farther than mere threats? I wondered. *Might she have been distressed enough to kill someone like Mrs. Milbourn?*

"You mentioned the murder..." she said, and her face lost some color as she frowned. "I am sorry to admit that Mrs. Milbourn... Well, she was an old friend of mine. We haven't spoken in many years, but I did know her well when she first began to be recognized for her work. Regardless..." She sighed. "I confess that whole tragedy really puts my own frustrations into perspective. While I might find my son's situation terribly unfair, at least he is still with us."

I blinked at her, and wondered if she was truly as sincere as she seemed. Someone covering up a murder would naturally want to appear as reasonable and sympathetic as possible, wouldn't they? My instincts whispered that she was likely telling the truth, and yet, I had cause to know how easily a person could play a role for reasons of her own...

"I am, in a way, glad the horrible business didn't happen under my watch," she said, shaking her head.

Then she turned to look at me, her expression softening.

"I will speak with the rest of the board, if they will see me," she said. "I have fences to mend there on my own behalf, and I shall put in a good word for you, too."

Our conversation wound down after that, and I bid her farewell. I made certain to avoid any chance for her to ask for my address or any information; her word of mouth could come and go, and she would have done as she said. They need not ever hear from a Miss Meadows.

I slipped into the back of the car a short while later, considering.

"Did you learn anything?" Miles asked, seemingly already reading the answer on my face.

"Not as much as I'd hoped," I said, my heart sinking. "Either that woman is an excellent liar or I have another name to scratch off my list of suspects."

9

"Miss Sylvia?"

I stopped at the sound of Miles' voice. I had hoped by now it wouldn't startle me as much as it did, but it mattered little, it seemed, that he had been working as our family's butler for almost a full month now. I looked around and found him at the top of the staircase, just as Joan and I were approaching it.

A few days had come and gone, where I had spent little time considering Mrs. Milbourn's death. I had little chance, between the first few sittings I had done for Mr. Steeles, along with a number of luncheons where my mother insisted Joan and I join her. I barely had time to think, let alone try and solve a murder with so little evidence.

Joan had begun to chide me about not getting at

least a name of some of the other board members, or having used a *real* name so that Mrs. Leavens might have introduced them. I hadn't considered anything past speaking with Mrs. Leavens at the time, and so, had not even come up with a plan as to what to do afterward.

"It's like chess, Sylvie," Joan had said. *"You have to think of all your options, what will or might happen, even if it never does."*

She was right...and I was regretting being so short-sighted.

"Yes?" I said, tucking a strand of hair behind my ear; Joan had convinced me to have it cut stylishly short only a few months ago and I still wasn't entirely used to it.

Miles bowed his head. "Mr. Adams is here to see you. To take you out for a stroll, in fact."

I frowned. "He is here? Now?" I asked.

Joan gave me a bit of a push, grinning at me. "Well, don't keep him waiting!" she said.

"But I – " I said.

She offered me a wave as she hurried down the stairs. "Have fun, Sylvie!" And she disappeared around the corner, heading toward the parlor.

Miles stood there, waiting for me to move.

Reluctantly, I started forward, and he led the way.

How have I gotten myself into a position where Mr. Adams now feels comfortable calling on me, uninvited? I wondered. *I have never been terribly enthusiastic about him, and my slowness to realize that has only encouraged him.*

"Miles?" I asked, stopping halfway down the staircase. I had come to a sudden decision. "Please inform Mr. Adams that I simply do not have the time to leave the house today."

"Is there a reason I should give?" he asked.

I thought quickly. "Tell him that I have a prior engagement," I said.

Miles nodded, and turned to go. He didn't question me any further, to my relief.

I hurried back up the stairs and around the corner of the hall, waiting.

I could barely make out the conversation, but heard Miles answer the door.

"Mr. Adams, I am terribly sorry to say that Miss Sylvia is otherwise engaged today," Miles said.

"Is she?" Mr. Adams asked. "Might I ask with what?"

"She did not say," Miles said. "Though I imagine it has something to do with her mother. She has been quite keen on taking Miss Sylvia around to a number of luncheons with her friends lately. I think Mr. Shipman's absence has made her rather lonely."

"I see..." Mr. Adams said. "And do you know, by any chance, if these luncheons are for other young ladies, such as Miss Sylvia and her sister?"

I narrowed my eyes, even though he couldn't see me. *As if it is any of his business whether there are gentlemen present at these luncheons. As if I have no right to dine with whomever I please.*

"I fear I am not privy to such information," Miles said.

"...Yes, I suppose not," Mr. Adams said. "Well, please tell Miss Sylvia I was asking after her, and to give me a call or send me a note letting me know how she has been feeling."

"Certainly, sir, I will make sure she hears," Miles said. "Good day."

The door closed, and I slumped against the wall, relieved. For a moment there, I had been afraid he would not go. Joan would be irritated at me, of course, for passing up this chance, but it was my decision to make, not hers.

I heard footsteps on the stairs, and then Miles appeared, looking mildly amused. "Never fear, Miss Sylvia. I sent him on his way."

"Did he look offended?" I asked.

"Oh, he didn't seem too put out," Miles said. "I think he understands that a young lady may lead a busy social life and be occupied with many engagements that leave her unavailable on short notice."

"Did he say when he might be back?" I asked.

"No," Miles said. "Shall I go after him and ask?"

"No," I said, hurriedly. "No, that's quite all right."

He nodded. "Very well, then. Is there anything else you'll be needing, Miss Sylvia? Or shall I go and see if your mother needs me?"

The question seemed simple enough, but it *felt* more pointed. He was asking if I wanted to confide in him. Somehow, I knew that. But did I dare discuss things with him, knowing what I now did of his past? Or at least suspecting what I did?

I looked at him, *really* looked at him for a moment. He seemed content to allow me to search his gaze, not shying away from it in the least.

What am I looking for? An answer? The truth? I wondered. *Why is it that I feel like I can trust him, despite his past? Why does it seem as if those two things cannot overlap?*

I knew I could never trust a murderer. If he really had been responsible for killing that woman back in England...a woman who might have been his wife, no less...

I looked away. I didn't have the answers yet, but I couldn't bring myself to ask.

"Would you please prepare the parlor for me?" I asked, glancing just past him down the stairs. "Mr. Steeles is coming this afternoon for my portrait, and I would like to have the place ready before he arrives."

"Certainly," he said, bowing his head. "Just as we had it set up last time?"

"Yes, thank you," I said. "Oh, and if you could find a

stool with a cushion this time, I know he would be most appreciative."

He nodded and started toward the stairs.

One thing was certain, I knew, staring after him. Whenever I looked at the handsome and perfectly acceptable Mr. Adams, it left me disappointed. *Is that because of Miles?* I wondered. There was no denying that our previous adventures had left me feeling some level of connection with Miles that I seemed unable to find with Mr. Adams.

"You know, Miss Sylvia..."

I looked up. "What is it?" I asked.

Miles' expression became cool. "Perhaps it is not my place to ask...but I have begun to wonder, as I am certain the rest of your family has, if you are thinking of accepting an offer soon?"

"An offer of what?" I asked, then my thoughts caught up with my question. "Marriage?"

"You have been seeing quite a few eligible young men as of late," Miles said, turning to lift a vase from a long table along the wall. He swept his bare hand along the polished surface beneath, no doubt looking to make sure the maids had been doing their jobs. "I imagine a good match would make your father happy."

"I – " I began, and my face grew warm. "I don't see how any of this is your business."

"I never said that it was," he said, his tone flat. "I am merely making conversation."

Of all the things he could discuss with me, this *is what he chooses?* I thought. *And why does he seem so intent to ask, yet so indifferent in his answers?*

I shook my head and stalked past him, annoyance growing within me that I could hardly pinpoint. What did it matter to him if men were suddenly taking an interest in me? It was high time, given my age and my family name. There was nothing unusual in it.

A nagging doubt at the back of my mind assured me that wasn't what had upset me.

Why did he care? Why did he feel the need to point it out?

"Miss Sylvia…" he said in a low voice.

I stopped at the top of the stairs, and turned to face him with a glare that Joan would have surely been proud to see. "What is it?" I asked, more sharply than necessary.

"After Mr. Steeles has come and gone, and you have some amount of free time, I would like to take you to meet someone," he said.

I blinked at him, surprised by the request. Was this the real reason he had wanted to speak with me?

"Who do you want me to meet?" I asked.

"Someone who might have answers for your investigation," he said.

My frustration melted away immediately. "Is this about one of your connections?" I asked. "Have they found something?"

He nodded, his eyes sweeping down the hall. A servant had just left one of the rooms at the very end – Joan's, it seemed – arms laden with linens and humming merrily.

"That is welcome news," I said. "I had begun to think that..."

"That you would never find the answer?"

The pointed look he gave me once again told me there was so much more to what he said. *I only wish he would tell me what it is!* I fumed in my thoughts.

"If you are willing, we can go to meet him this evening, after dinner," he said.

I knew Joan would question me. "What of my family?" I asked.

"None of them know that you do not have plans with Mr. Adams, do they?" he asked. "It wouldn't hurt to allow them to make their own assumptions."

He had come up with that solution awfully quickly. The small hairs on the back of my neck stood up. Did deception come so naturally to him, then?

"Or here is a better idea, instead," he continued. "We shall tell your family that I'm going to visit an old friend of mine, as this is my evening off. You are accompanying me so that you might give my friend the chance to take a look at your violin."

"My violin? But why?" I asked.

Miles smiled. "My friend has a hobby of repairing musical instruments. I noticed that scratch along the back of your violin recently. I thought you might like him to take a look at it and see what he can do."

I hesitated. "That is very thoughtful, Miles," I said, unable to fully comprehend everything that had happened in the past few minutes. The pendulum of my emotions had been working overtime, swaying this way and that, back and forth –

For the moment, though...

For the moment...

"Well?" he asked.

"All right," I said. "It is a plan. We will go and see what we can learn from your friend this evening."

He smiled. "Good. I shall make the arrangements."

For the moment...I would choose to trust him.

10

"You seem surprised," Miles said, turning to grin at me over his shoulder in the car.

I peered out the window up at a handsome rowhouse no more than half a mile away from my home. In a respectable neighborhood, no less. "Mr. and Mrs. Fern live in this house just to the right," I said. "We came here last Christmas."

"I am certain my friend knows them," Miles said.

I looked hard at him. "How do you know this man?" I asked.

"We have been friends for many years," he said. "You can trust what he says."

"And was he once living on the streets, as you did?" I asked.

Miles' smile grew. "A fair question. No, he never was. In fact, your father likely knows him."

"But not me?" I asked.

"You might recognize his name," Miles said. "Shall we go in and see him?"

"I suppose," I said.

"Don't forget your violin," Miles said.

We made our way up the stairs, and were soon greeted.

"Mr. Miles, what a pleasant surprise," the butler said with a wide grin.

Miles returned it easily. "It's just Miles, Bernard, just Miles."

"Well, come in, come in," Bernard said, sweeping us in over the threshold. "When I was told that you were coming this evening, I could hardly believe it. I would have thought you had made your way back to London by now."

"No," Miles said. "Ah, Bernard, this is Miss Sylvia Shipman."

"What a pleasure it is, Miss," Bernard said. "Might I take your coat?"

I allowed him, studying Miles.

He seemed an entirely different person, and it greatly surprised me to see such a jovial reaction from the butler. Miles, it seemed, had not been lying about knowing this man for some time.

"Where is my friend?" Miles asked.

"Where he always is," Bernard said, peering out from the coat closet. "Go on, show yourself in."

Miles gestured for me to climb the stairs first, which I did with a modicum of apprehension. What, or who, was I to find?

The house was handsome, minimal yet comfortable. It seemed that Miles' acquaintance, despite living in one of the best neighborhoods in the city, cared little for the more expensive sorts of pieces. It made the whole place feel homier, in truth.

"Is he married?" I asked, looking at door after door, wondering what lay beyond.

"Yes," Miles said. "Has five children, as well. From what he told me, they've gone ahead of him to their cottage in Upstate, where they will spend Thanksgiving and Christmas this year. Taking some time away from the city."

If he had a family, then it was more and more likely that I knew who this person was, too.

Miles took a turn at the end of the hall, revealing another staircase. Much narrower than the one in the foyer, it seemed to be used more for the servants. A single door stood at the very top.

Miles pushed it open, and brilliant golden light flooded out onto the steps.

"What a pleasure to see you," came a voice from within.

Miles stepped aside to let me pass, and I found a man I hardly recognized at first. I blinked once or twice and then it struck me.

"Mr. Daniels?" I asked, gaping.

Mr. Daniels, a man with a great deal less hair than I remembered, stood near the fireplace. "Hello, Miss Shipman."

I took a step toward him. "You and Miles know each other? But how is that possible?"

It seemed a very unlikely friendship, inconsistent with anything I knew of Miles' life, past or present.

Mr. Daniels didn't answer the question, merely giving me a gentle smile. Immediately I was taken back to the Christmas that I turned seven.

"How long has it been since we last met?" I asked, and suddenly, I realized the home itself had been trying to tell me precisely who it was that it belonged to. I should have known it, in the paintings of the horses on the wall, in the worn bridle hanging near the stairs, in the bronze sculptures and the handmade pieces of furniture, all of which were imperfect. "A dozen years? Maybe more?"

His smile widened. "It would have to have been, given that the last time I saw you, you were but a child."

I grinned. "And your wife? And children? How are they?"

He gave me a small nod. "All fine. Lydia is out for the afternoon, acquiring what she can for our children...and grandchildren."

I gasped. "You have grandchildren? Are they Peter's?"

He nodded again. "And Lily's. Both were married last year, and Lily just had her baby a few weeks ago. They've all gone to our estate. I suppose you wouldn't remember it, as young as you were, but – "

"The stables," I said, my eyes widening. "Why, it is one of my most cherished memories of Christmas. I remember walking through the most handsome stable I ever saw. Garlands had been strung from the rafters overhead, candles burned in glass orbs on each post, the horses adorned with bright red ribbons." I laughed. "The best thing about that night was the candy canes given to my sister and me at the door, even before we had come inside."

He laughed, too. "That was Lydia's idea. A way to keep the children entertained for a moment while all the parents greeted one another. It worked, as well. By the time you had all had your fill, dinner was ready." His eyes twinkled. "I remember it well."

As did I. I looked around. "I can see Mrs. Daniels' touch everywhere," I said. "With her love of horses."

He followed my gaze. "It's true. She managed to find the most tasteful pieces, many of which she has had commissioned based on some of the horses we have owned in the past. Her favorite, perhaps you might recall, was a red mare named Flame. Lydia adored her and was devastated when she passed." He turned and gestured to an enormous canvas hanging above the fireplace.

I stared at it. A lush green field, brilliant blue sky, thousands of yellow wildflowers...and a copper red horse bolting through it as free as the day itself. "It looks...so real," I said. "As if I might reach my hand out and touch her."

"I had this made for her in remembrance of Flame," Mr. Daniels said.

It surprised me that I myself felt a genuine sadness. "I'm so sorry," I said. "I imagine she loves this piece."

"That she does," Mr. Daniels said. "But I know you are not here to speak of horses, though I am certain that could be done once we have completed our business?"

I blinked at him, dazed for a brief moment...before I turned around to see Miles standing near the door, watching me closely. "Oh, I – " I began. "Of course. Yes. My apologies."

"Please, have a seat," Mr. Daniels said, gesturing to an overstuffed tufted chair beside the fireplace. "You as well, Nicholas."

I glanced over my shoulder just in time to catch Miles give Mr. Daniels a rather pointed look before joining me in the matching chair beside me.

"My apologies, it's Miles these days, isn't it?" Mr. Daniels asked.

I glanced back and forth between them. "How is it that you know each other?" I asked.

"We have known one another for years," Mr. Daniels answered, though I caught another look between the pair of them. "It's an old habit to break when you have known someone for so long." He stood near the fireplace, leaning against the mantle.

I surveyed Miles, who seemed intent on watching Mr. Daniels. It seemed the obvious questions would not be answered, and I would remain once again in the dark. "Why don't you tell Miss Sylvia what you have told me?" Miles asked.

"Certainly," Mr. Daniels said. "When Miles here informed me that you had taken up a little sleuthing, I have to admit I was a bit surprised. I might have expected something of the sort from your sister, as unpredictable as she is, but then again, you always seemed to pay close attention to those around you, even as a child."

"I did?" I asked.

"You have an eye for observing people, even if they aren't quite aware," he said. "Anyway, I was all too happy to help you in your endeavor."

"Really?" I asked. "I assume Miles informed you of what has happened?"

He nodded. "Indeed. I read about it in the paper myself. Very troubling, as any intentional killing would be, but this one got me thinking..."

"How so?" I asked.

"I know quite a few people who were there at the event," Mr. Daniels said. "My wife is a personal friend of Mrs. Waters, a family that I know you are familiar with as well."

I nodded. "Yes, I am friends with her daughter."

"Well, we heard from her a few little details the museum staff has not shared with the general public. For example, it has been discovered that a purse belonging to Mrs. Milbourn was stolen at the scene of the crime. She had been seen with it, even given a guest at the gallery something from within, so there were multiple accounts of its presence, but when the police were looking for identification after her death, there was none to be found."

"So the purse is missing?" I asked.

"Well, not anymore," Mr. Daniels said. "As it turns out, the purse has since been found."

I straightened. That was a surprise, because I was already beginning to think that would be my next task. "Who has it?" I asked.

"Her name is Ida Turner," he said.

"I don't think I'm familiar with her," I said.

"Likely not. With her station in life, I do not believe she is someone your parents would have crossed paths with. There is one small problem, however..." he said.

"She's gone into hiding," Miles finished for him.

My brow furrowed. "Hiding? Then how did you find out about her?"

"Well, there are very few people who know," he said. "I happen to be one of three – well, now five, I suppose, with the pair of you – and she has gone to great lengths to make sure no one comes looking for her. However, we've heard rumor of where she might be found."

"How is that possible?" I asked. "Was it not the police that found her out?"

"No," Mr. Daniels said. "Which is the tricky thing."

Miles turned to me. "Miss Turner is terrified, as you might imagine, that she will be accused of killing Mrs. Milbourn."

"And I'm assuming she claims she didn't?" I asked. "I take it someone doesn't believe her?"

"No one quite knows," Mr. Daniels said. "From what I have heard of her, Ida wouldn't be capable of something like that."

"This is where you come in," Miles said. "I told Mr. Daniels you would be the one who could persuade her to talk, or at least to go to the police with anything she knows.

"So when you said you had a lead for me, you meant for me to look into it?" I asked. "Isn't that a bit deceptive?"

"Not at all," Miles said, as casually as if I were no

more than teasing him. "In fact, I thought you would see it as proof of my utmost faith in you."

My eyes narrowed slightly, but I turned back to Mr. Daniels. "Very well, then. What of your opinion, Mr. Daniels? Have you agreed to tell me all this with the hopes that I might go and speak with her?"

"That is entirely up to you," he said. "I have no control in regards to your decision hereafter. I have simply provided the information. It will be your choice what to do with it, I suppose."

I looked back at Miles. "Why do you think I could convince her?" I asked. "And what exactly am I convincing her of?"

"To come clean about whatever she knows, naturally," Miles said.

"About the murder?" I asked. "Is she aware of any details?"

"I know nothing of that," Mr. Daniels said. "Only that she obviously fears she will be accused of the killing."

"Why would she have stolen the purse in the first place?" I asked, knowing full well that neither of them would know for certain.

"It could be any number of reasons," Miles said. "Perhaps she thought there would be cash or valuables in it. It's entirely possible she was simply at the wrong place at the wrong time."

"I tend to agree," Mr. Daniels said. "Theft seems an

unlikely additional risk for the person who went to such painstaking lengths to kill Mrs. Milbourn. The murder was something personal, but the theft could have been random and unrelated."

"The killing was planned, it would have to have been," Miles said. "The murderer obviously knew the gallery well, knew *her* well, and likely went in specifically to end her life. The moment would have to have been perfect for them to be able to get away with it unseen."

"And you think stealing the purse would make it too easy to connect the thief to the murder," I said. "An unnecessary risk that they could be caught literally holding the bag."

"The killer would be too smart to do that," Miles said. "They will have done everything they could to eliminate any connection to them."

"All right," I said. "So why, if we think she is *not* the murderer, should I go and speak with this Ida Turner?"

"She might be able to give you information," Mr. Daniels said. "She was close on hand immediately before or after the stabbing, possibly closer than anyone else. Perhaps she saw more, heard more, and could point you in the right direction... There are any number of things she might tell you, which she has refused to share with others."

I sighed. "I suppose this is the best lead I have had thus far," I said.

"I would advise you to be vigilant," Mr. Daniels said. "Even Mr. Waters has little knowledge about all this and wants to keep the matter quiet. I imagine the killer will be keeping a close eye on him and his family. You can see why he would be uneasy, reluctant to directly involve himself or speak to the authorities more than necessary."

"Which is why this would be a good alternative way to go," Miles said. "Someone no one is watching, like you, can more safely ask questions. As long as you are careful not to attract the wrong attention."

I nodded. "That makes sense to me."

"Matthew, did you by any chance – " Miles asked.

"Yes, it's on the bed in the guest room upstairs," Mr. Daniels said. "Feel free to go and fetch it."

Miles nodded, before rising and heading out of the room.

I watched him go. *What could he want from Mr. Daniels?* I wondered.

"Care for some coffee?" Mr. Daniels asked, turning to a buffet table along the back wall, almost in the same place where ours was kept in our own home. Some stylistic choices never seemed to change.

"Yes..." I said. "Thank you."

A quiet settled over the room, and I debated asking precisely what Miles was going to fetch. But I suspected I might be told, in politer language, that it was none of my business. Instead, I decided to ask about Miles himself.

"You were saying that you and Miles have known each other for some time," I said. "How did you two meet?"

"Oh, we have mutual friends," he said, his back still turned to me as he poured the still steaming coffee from a ceramic carafe. "Our paths crossed a few times at various parties and dinners, that sort of thing." He glanced at me over his shoulder. "How do you take your coffee? Milk? Any sugar?"

"A little sugar," I said. "And yes, milk as well."

He nodded, turning away.

I wanted to ask more, to find out what I could while I had the chance. I felt I could trust Mr. Daniels, but how did I know that I could trust Miles?

"I suppose my family knows so little about him," I said. My heart skipped, as I realized I was giving too much away. There was no need to share the hand I'd had in how Miles had come into our employ. Even my own family didn't seem to realize I had more or less hired him, without consulting anyone. "Right now, of course," I added quickly. "As new as he is to our household and all that."

Mr. Daniels set the carafe down and hesitated for the briefest of moments, which gave me pause. "Well..." he said, finally turning around with a cup of fresh coffee in each hand, a smile on his face. "Allow me to assuage any worries you might have."

He set the cup down in front of me, and took the chair Miles had been sitting in.

"Miles is perhaps one of the most dependable men I have ever known," he said. "A true and loyal friend, when one is needed."

"Really?" I asked.

He nodded. "I suppose I could be biased, but I believe he has great generosity, which too many people have taken advantage of. He has been hurt but has come through the better for it. I am proud to call him my friend, and you can rest assured he will serve your family well."

I nodded. "Well...thank you, Mr. Daniels. You have given me a great deal more confidence in him." I cleared my throat, drawing the coffee to my lips. "I am certain it will please my father to know you have such a high opinion of Miles."

"I would be more than happy to tell him myself," Mr. Daniels said with another grin, holding his coffee aloft in a cheer. "I think it is high time I gave your father a call and we all made plans to get together again as families."

"I think he would like that very much," I said, sipping the coffee. The hot, sweet liquid coated my tongue, with just enough bitterness to balance it. A much darker, deeper roast than what I was used to, it tickled my senses and I knew at once that Mr. Daniels must have a very specific way he enjoyed his drink, far more precise than how Gibbins made it for my family.

"I know so little about Miles, and where he comes from," I tried again. Those questions still lingered in my mind. "I know he comes from London, but I know nothing of his family, who he might have left behind..." I looked at my host over the rim of my cup and waited.

Mr. Daniels looked away, clearing his throat. "Every man has a story," he said, rising to his feet. "And Miles' is for him to share, and not me."

My heart sank as I drew another sip from the cup, much bitterer this time.

"He wishes to keep his past in the past," Mr. Daniels continued. "And I respect his desires."

He is intentionally being elusive, I thought. *The both of them are. Am I never to learn the truth of what happened with Miles? With his wife?*

I debated asking any further, but Miles returned just a moment later. "What? Having coffee without me?"

Mr. Daniels grinned. "I'm surprised you have developed a taste for the stuff," he said, setting his cup down to retrieve one for Miles. "Not two years ago, you despised it."

"But never the smell," Miles said. "Which I loved."

Mr. Daniels thrust a cup into his hands. “You’re an odd one.”

Miles laughed, and then he drew Mr. Daniels’ attention to my violin, which Mr. Daniels said he was happy to look at.

As our kind host examined the scratched instrument, I allowed my thoughts to wander.

If Mr. Daniels says I can trust Miles, then I can set my fears aside...can’t I? I thought. I trusted Mr. Daniels, and he thought Miles was dependable. Therefore...

Then why can’t I shake this worry?

11

"I will be right here if you need me," Miles said as he turned off the engine of the car. He turned around in his seat. "Although you really don't need to do this alone."

I stared at him. When we had left Mr. Daniels' home, I had declared that I would be the one to go and speak with Ida Turner. I did not think I needed, much less wanted, help.

Even though Mr. Daniels had said what he had about Miles, assuring me that I could trust him, I still found I couldn't shake those nagging doubts. If he had been willing to share anything about Miles' past, anything at all, I might have felt differently. But as both men were clearly hiding something...

"Perhaps I have changed my mind," I said, reconsidering nonetheless. "I went alone last time. I think it might be helpful to have you along with me."

He requires watching, I decided. *And I cannot watch him, if I avoid his company.*

He brightened. "You're sure?" he asked.

"Yes, I think it would be good to have another set of ears in the room. Perhaps you will be able to catch something I miss." That, and a woman who had stolen a purse certainly seemed more likely to be one who might attack me without much thought. It might be wise not to be alone with her.

"I would be honored," he said. "We should not delay. The day grows late, and I don't want to be late for dinner. Your father has quite taken to my accompanying him."

I smirked. "You mean when he has the chance to tell you everything he doesn't wish to do for the rest of the evening?"

A mischievous grin appeared on his face. "Why, it is my job, Miss Sylvia. I am all too happy to do as he asks of me."

He slipped out of the car, still wearing the smile.

Miss Turner happened to be staying at the south end of the city, less than a mile from the end of the peninsula. I had hardly traversed to this side of town, mostly out of worry of the stories I'd heard. Father had forbidden Joan and me from ever setting foot down here, and while Joan wished to tempt fate more than once, I never had the desire.

I certainly would not have called it undesirable, but the broken window in the last rowhouse across the street did nothing to settle my sensitive nerves.

I noticed Miles' sweeping gaze along the street, the hard set of his jaw.

I quickened my steps, and hurried up the stairs to the door.

I saw a column of names beside the door, each of which had a button next to them. There were ten in all. I found the name I was looking for second from the bottom. Kurkland.

Miles stepped up beside me and jabbed the button with his thumb. A horrendous screech pierced the otherwise quiet stoop.

"Pardon me, but is Mr. Kurkland in?" Miles asked, apparently undeterred by the noise.

Another sharp blare, brief but enough to send chills down my spine, followed by static. No voice answered.

Miles glanced at me.

"This is the correct place, right?" I asked, looking around. "Or is it possible there is another Kurkland – "

A crackle burst from the speaker. "This is Kurkland. Who am I speaking to?"

"A servant of the Shipman family. I am here accompanying a Miss Shipman. There is something she would like to speak with you about."

Static answered for more than a few seconds before the voice of Mr. Kurkland came back on. "Shipman, you say?" he asked. "Business?"

"You might say that," said Miles.

"Very well. You may enter."

A harsh note like a car horn alerted us to the door unlocking, and Miles pulled the door open for me.

We stepped inside, and my stomach turned. The staircase, splintered and warped, might have been the cleanest part of the entrance hall. The carpet that stretched across the floor boasted moth-eaten holes and threadbare patches. The wallpaper peeled back at the corners, and the first door on my left had scratch marks gathered mostly around the doorknob.

"Let's not dawdle," Miles said in a low voice. He gestured toward the stairs, and he and I walked side by side up to the next floor.

Kurkland's level looked in somewhat better shape than the one downstairs, but the same worn wood seemed flimsy and unreliable. I certainly wouldn't have wanted to stay a single night in a place like this.

"Let's take this slow and cautious," Miles said. "Do we have a story to tell him?"

I appreciated his decision to ask me instead of just going in and assuming I would follow along. "I think it safest to stick as close to the truth as possible," I said. "Less chance of being tripped up."

"Perhaps I should introduce you as a private investigator?" Miles asked. "It might make him more willing to talk."

I hesitated. "I suppose, if it will help...although it's not exactly true. I have no license, no training – "

"Have you solved a crime?" he asked.

"Well – technically, yes, but – "

"And have you managed to discover the identity of a murderer?" he asked.

I hesitated again. These seemed like trick questions all of a sudden. "I have, but – "

"Then it is accurate enough," he said, taking a step toward the door.

"It wasn't without help," I said. "That much should be obvious by the fact that you are here with me."

"True," he said. "But I highly doubt a private investigator has ever lived who has not had help at one time or another."

He knocked on the door, and a small slat above a tiny lookout hole in the door slid open. A pair of eyes shone out, so grey they were almost silver. "What is it you really want with me?" he asked. "I'm not fool enough to think you would have come here for business when you could have easily come to my factory and sat with me in my office."

"You are a perceptive man, I see," Miles said. He

inclined his head toward me. "We have come to help. We're aware of a particular...guest of yours, who is in bad circumstances, needing the sort of assistance that only a private investigator can provide."

I straightened as the silvery eyes turned to me.

"Private investigator?" he asked, his gaze sharpening. "Excuse me."

The slat snapped shut, leaving Miles and I alone again.

Footsteps on the staircase behind us startled me. A woman laughed, and a couple passed by on their way up the steps. He staggered slightly, and she giggled into his shoulder.

"I suspect he has gone to inform her that you are here," Miles said under his breath.

"Isn't he going to wonder how in the world we found out about her?" I asked.

"Oh, that's most certainly going to be something they ask us about," he said.

A chain rattled on the other side of the door, followed by a *shink* of metal on wood. A moment later, the door flew open to reveal the rest of the man those silver eyes belonged to. Of average height and lean, he had short hair that almost perfectly matched the shade of his grey eyes. He gazed at Miles and me in the doorway, but said nothing until we had stepped inside and he had closed the door behind us.

"I want to hear how much you know before I allow

you to take another step into my home," Mr. Kurkland said.

Miles glanced at me.

"I know you are housing your cousin," I said. "Ida Turner. I know she has gone into hiding after rumor has it she snatched a purse belonging to Mrs. Milbourn after her death."

A flash in Mr. Kurkland's eyes was all I needed for confirmation. He stiffened, and cleared his throat. "I suppose you already know too much for me to try and deny it," he said. "Though I have no idea how you came by that information."

"We have friends all over," Miles said. "And their friends know the right sort for information, you see."

Mr. Kurkland paled slightly. "I suppose a private investigator would have those sorts of connections," he said. He nodded. "Very well. I have told her you are here, and..." He sighed. "She's a bit relieved that you found her."

That was certainly not what I expected to hear.

He led us to a room at the back of the house, which boasted furnishings that were quite out of place in an apartment as run down as the rest of the building. It saddened me, seeing pieces that were past their prime, housed in such tired surroundings.

He stopped at a room that had no door, covered simply by a curtain. One might have walked right past it had he not gestured to it.

I pushed it aside, and my heart sank even further.

It couldn't have been any bigger than a closet at my own home, no more than a few feet wide on either side. A child's bed had been pushed into the corner, leaving little room for the trunk at the foot of it. There was also a low, narrow table stacked high with boxes, a few bowls, and a lamp.

A woman stood at the far side, which really was not all that far from us, her arms wrapped tightly around her boney frame. The shawl draped over her shoulders reminded me of the wings of a bat, and trembled slightly in the frigid room; the brick wall beside me clearly was the outermost wall of the building, and the cold pressed in through the thin barrier. She seemed as frail as her surroundings, with dark, thin hair that had been cut at jagged angles around her face, likely done by herself.

"Are you here to help me?" she asked, her face turned hopefully up to mine. She clutched her hands together as she took the two steps to cross the room to me, and I saw that she stood nearly a head shorter than I.

"Are you Miss Turner?" I asked.

She nodded, rather exaggeratedly. "I have been hoping you would find me – or at least, that *someone* would!" She let out a laugh, and tears welled in her eyes. "I have been here for – for *days* now, uncertain what to do, if I should even leave the house! I know my own home has been watched by the police – " Her eyes widened as she surveyed me. "If *you've* found me, then surely the police won't be far behind?"

"I cannot speak for them, Miss Turner, as I am not working with them," I said.

"Yes, I explained to her who you are," Mr. Kurkland said from out in the hall.

"I didn't recognize your name," Miss Turner said, her already wide eyes growing wider, as round as an owl's. "Miss...Ship-something?"

"Shipman," I said. "And I doubt we would have many mutual acquaintances."

"The important thing is that she's got a knack for handling difficult matters," Miles put in, nodding to me. "She solved her own uncle's murder, if that gives you any peace of mind."

"Your own uncle?" Miss Turner asked. "That does relieve my mind..." She appeared to cheer up a little.

I worried that the woman's distracted way of speaking might make it slightly more difficult to find the truth I was looking for.

"I must admit I was surprised that someone knew where I was," Miss Turner said, turning around to sink down onto the foot of her tiny bed. "I only told one other person where I was going."

"I suppose word travels," I said. "However, you are glad that we've found you now? Why?"

"To prove my innocence, of course," she said,

staring at me as if I had suggested the sky was anything other than blue.

I hesitated. She looked at me with such intensity, and yet such clarity, that it was tempting to take her at her word. That would be a foolish thing to do, though, and that meant I would need to dig around in her head just a little more.

"Miss Turner," I began. "Is it true that you stole the purse of the woman who was killed at the art exhibit?"

Miss Turner reached over the trunk at the end of the bed, pulled the top open, and pointed inside.

"It's right there," she said. "The red one."

I stared at the handbag lying inside the trunk, amongst unfolded sweaters and a handsome bowler hat with a compromised crown squashed in on itself. I eyed the purse nervously, as if it might bite my hand if I reached for it.

"Go on, you can look at it," Miss Turner said.

Carefully, I picked it up. The leather, cool beneath my fingers, had been worn along the fold at the top, and the brass button clasping it shut had been tarnished from what must have been years of use.

I glanced over my shoulder at Miles, whose brow had wrinkled, his green eyes fixed on the bag in my hand.

I swallowed, and slowly lifted the clasp.

I didn't know what I expected to find within, but my heart sank when I realized my expectations had been too high. It seemed the woman hardly kept a thing inside; a lipstick tube, a money clip with no more than a few bills, and a slim, black book.

I pulled the book out and flipped open the pages... only to find nothing written upon them.

"Disappointing, isn't it?" asked Miss Turner, her lips scrunched beneath her nose. "I had hoped to find a diary or some such. But not a thing."

"Is this what you found inside?" Miles asked. "You haven't tampered with anything in it?"

"Of course not," Miss Turner said.

"You didn't take any of the money or anything like that?" I asked.

She shook her head, her chin lifting. "Honestly, you would think me no better than a common thief."

I glanced at Miles, and then Mr. Kurkland.

"My cousin has a slight...problem," Mr. Kurkland said.

"I have all the money I need," Miss Turner said. "It isn't about that." Her eyes then went vacant, glassy, and a lopsided grin bloomed on her lips.

Goosebumps popped up all down my arms.

"This feeling comes over me..." she said, her voice higher, wispier. "This...*desire.* It's like an itch I can't scratch, an ache I can't soothe... It urges me to take things. To prove to myself just how *easy* it really is..."

"It's the thrill of it that enthralls you," Miles observed.

Miss Turner seemed to return to her own mind, her head swiveling around to him. She blinked at him. "Well, I suppose that's it. I simply cannot control it."

"Mrs. Milbourn's purse is one of dozens she has managed to steal," Mr. Kurkland said, eyeing Miss Turner as if she were no more than a naughty child. He raised a brow likewise at her. "All of which have been returned to their rightful owners."

"No one ever knows it was me," Miss Turner said with a smug grin, laying her hand delicately against her heart. "Well, *almost* no one. In my earlier days I was a bit less graceful."

"Why did you take Mrs. Milbourn's?" I asked. "And how? When?"

"So many questions..." Miss Turner said with a *tsk, tsk, tsk.* "Well, what was I supposed to do, hmm? It was just *lying* there on the floor, just *begging* to be grabbed!"

"You mean the night of the murder?" Miles asked.

"Yes, precisely," Miss Turner said.

My brows furrowed. "And you thought nothing of going to take it, while Mrs. Milbourn was lying collapsed there?"

"You make it sound as if I am some monstrous, heartless person," Miss Turner said with a frown. "I didn't know the woman from Adam, and in the midst of the commotion, with the idea that I might get caught – " She visibly shivered, and laughed with great mirth. "Oh, it was simply *too much* to pass up!"

I stared at her in disbelief. "Miss Turner, your actions are more serious than you seem to realize."

She straightened. "I will have you know that I am fully aware of myself," she said. "So much so that I knew if someone found me with the purse they would accuse me of her murder. Of course, I didn't think of this until *after* I had sneaked away with it. Nevertheless, I didn't want her death pinned on me."

Miles folded his arms. "You are going to try and tell us you *didn't* kill her?" he asked.

Miss Turner's expression was somewhat vacant. "Why would I so openly tell you I stole her purse, but *not* admit to the murder? Are they not both crimes?"

"One far more severe," Miles said.

"You didn't kill her?" I asked again.

"No," Miss Turner said. "I did not kill her."

"Then do you know who did?" I asked. "If you were near enough to see the purse, to get close to her – "

"No," Miss Turner said. "I saw nothing. I heard nothing, either. All I could think about was the purse, and making off with it."

I sighed, and looked back over at Miles, who shrugged.

"I suppose this was nothing more than a waste of time," he said.

Well, if we've learned nothing else, we now know there is seemingly nothing to learn here.

"I advise you to go to the police and confess all," I

told Miss Turner. "I'm afraid that's all the help I can give you. If you ever want to return to your own home again, if you ever want to get your life back to normal, you're going to have to persuade them your involvement and knowledge are minimal, so that they stop searching for you. You're guilty of theft but nothing worse."

"I've arranged for my cousin to see someone about her problem," Mr. Kurkland assured us. "She will get the help she needs."

Miss Turner said nothing to all of this, and I could see she was disappointed at my advice. Whether she would follow it, I didn't know, but I had told the truth when I said it was the only help I knew how to give her.

Miles and I left a few moments later.

"You did well," Miles said when we were outdoors again, as he pulled the car door open for me.

I shrugged. "I don't suppose I did very much," I said. "We haven't learned anything, apart from who *didn't* kill Mrs. Milbourn."

I slid into the backseat, and he closed the door and slipped into the front.

As we started off for home, I thought over our progress or lack of it. It had been easy enough to accept Ida Turner's story in the moment, when she was right in front of me. The woman seemed ignorant enough of the murder details.

But was I being too gullible, believing it was mere coincidence that she was at the scene, had stolen the victim's handbag, but had nothing to do with her death? What if she had played some sort of role in the killing and I simply couldn't see it? What if her kleptomania was nothing more than a ruse to create the appearance of innocence?

I admitted to myself that it was a possibility, and yet...it was difficult to imagine a woman like Miss Turner being clever or calculated enough to pull off what Mrs. Milbourn's killer had done and get away with it for all this time. It didn't add up.

I shook my head at my own musings. I had no choice but to proceed as if she was innocent, for the time being. If new evidence arose later to suggest otherwise, I would revisit the question...

12

I had one path left that I could think of. With the avenues of Miss Turner and Mrs. Leavens resulting in dead ends for now, I had to try and come up with another means of finding a suspect. I didn't want to contact Catherine or her father, worrying that it might draw the wrong kind of attention.

The idea that came to mind surprised me out of the blue the following morning, as my attentions had been distracted elsewhere.

"Good afternoon, Mr. Steeles," I said as the artist strode into the parlor, just as he had the three times he had visited before.

He beamed at me from the doorway, the canvas clutched beneath his arm. He inclined his head. "Miss Shipman, you are looking lovely, as always."

I smiled back, my tension easing ever so slightly.

He pulled out the small, round stool that had been tucked away beneath an end table, and set it in front of the easel that he had brought in with him. "I expect we are nearly done," he said, examining the canvas as he set it down. "Which makes me slightly sad, I must admit. You have to be one of the most patient subjects I have ever had, making nary a peep as I worked."

I found the same wingback chair that I had chosen for the portrait, a handsome green chair of velvet as soft as a rabbit. I settled myself down into it. "Really?" I asked. "Are they uncomfortable? Or do they just grow tired?"

"A little of both, I think," he said, peering at me around the side of the corner of the canvas. "But never mind about them. I think the end result we have here will be as exquisite as the subject."

My cheeks flushed, although I should have been used to exaggerated compliments by now. It seemed to be his way.

"Once I finish this today, I will be able to take it home and put the finishing touches on it," he said. "Now, turn your head to the side – yes, just like that, wonderful. Hold that pose for a few moments."

My heart began to quicken as his words sunk in. *The last session...that means this might be the last time I have the chance to question him. Which means...*I mused.

Which means I need to find a way to casually start talking to him again about Mrs. Milbourn.

I swallowed, my eyes locking for a moment onto Miles, who stood dutifully at one of Father's bookshelves, straightening his collection of old books from law school. The look Miles offered, though brief, seemed to be an attempt to embolden me. He gave a subtle nod before turning away.

I turned back to Mr. Steeles…or rather the back of his canvas. All I could see happened to be from his knees down, when he sat on his stool.

I straightened, and cleared my throat. "Perhaps this will be opening up old wounds…" I said, doing my best to keep everything but my mouth from moving. "But I heard that Mrs. Milbourn's funeral took place. They say it was a beautiful service."

For a moment, all I heard was the gentle scratch of the brush bristles on the canvas.

I didn't dare turn my head to look, but as we had agreed before Mr. Steeles' arrival, Miles stepped around the edge of the room to where he had a clear view of the artist. I could see Miles from where I sat, and as his eyes narrowed slightly, he glanced over at me and gave the slightest shake of his head.

No response, at least not visibly, I thought.

"Yes, I heard as much, too," Mr. Steeles said, seemingly indifferent. He leaned out around the canvas, waving the tip of his brush at me. "Shift your head slightly to the left, please. Good girl."

I did as he asked, glancing at Miles again.

He nodded toward Mr. Steeles, encouraging me onward.

"I imagine it would have been far too difficult for you to go," I said. "Given your relationship with her. I know you mentioned you were asked to speak there, and were uncertain whether you should go. I suppose that was a difficult decision to make."

Silence again.

I looked at Miles for answers. His brow furrowed, and I assumed he mirrored Mr. Steeles' face for me.

Well, that was certainly interesting. At least I read him right in that regard.

"Yes, well..." Mr. Steeles said, reaching for a jar of paint thinner. He swirled the brush inside it, and bright crimson swirled around in the clear liquid, like a cyclone of powdered rubies. "Perhaps I gave you the wrong idea of my thoughts on the woman."

My pulse quickened. "My apologies. I didn't mean to trouble you."

He sighed heavily, and Miles and I looked at one another, both curious. This didn't seem at all like how he had acted when he had spoken of her last. What had changed?

"She was indeed a mentor of mine," Mr. Steeles said, withdrawing his brush to press it into a dollop of green paint on his palette. "She saw great things in me, that is true... But it was not all flowers and sunshine..."

At once I thought of the look he and Mrs. Milbourn had exchanged during their encounter at the gallery. I had thought it was anger, at least initially. After speaking with him the first time, I had changed my perception that it might have been disappointment. It was clear something had gone unexplained. He had been vague, but overall his testimony of her had been positive.

"I hardly know a relationship that could be considered perfect," I said, and resisted the urge to glance at Miles.

"Yes, well..." Mr. Steeles' said, his voice a shade darker. "I should not bore you with the details."

I looked once again at Miles, who gave a small nod.

What did that mean? Should I press on? Or should I leave it as is?

No, I knew Miles well enough to know which he meant.

"I am sorry to hear that," I said. "As I said, I don't wish to dredge up old memories. It must be difficult for you to even think about. You must miss her something terrible."

He drew his knees closer together, both of which were suddenly stiff as boards. "I don't imagine she would have felt the same about me, had the situation been in reverse," he said. "I must have made it seem to you that she and I were close. When in the last three years or so, that couldn't be further from the truth. I did a commissioned piece for her, and she was dissatisfied with my work, and as such, never paid me for it. She has owed me for two and a half years now, and simply...stopped speaking to me after we had a nasty fight about the whole thing. She began to avoid me."

The corners of Miles' lips curled up, and he nodded to me.

Mr. Steeles peered around the edge of his portrait. He grinned at me, which seemed contrary to the mood he had just set. "Not that it mattered, really. I was not the only one she cheated or slighted. To be honest, I think she was going a bit senile. Forgot to do a lot of things, made some bad decisions with the board of the gallery, missed a number of appointments, I hear. Poor dear...it was heartbreaking, really."

My insides iced over, and I had to make sure a grimace didn't appear on my face. *His true resentment of her begins to bleed through,* I thought. For a moment, he had been as clear as a glass of water...the next, sidestepping and swiping a façade over the whole ordeal to hide the truth.

"Yes, she was a remarkable woman," he said, almost wistfully, the harshness in his tone nothing but a memory. "She will be sorely missed by many. Even me, I should think, in the end."

He recovered quickly, I could give him that. He had

thrown me off, enough that I questioned if I had really heard the animosity in his voice.

I could see just how false he was.

I had suspected it, though, from the very beginning. He was not the sort to trust.

"Well, that's it, I think," he said far too brightly now, hopping to his feet. He tilted his head, examining the canvas once more. He scratched his chin. "I think I have all I need. Now I shall take it back to my studio where I can make the finishing touches and frame it for you."

"Oh…all right," I said, trying not to frown in frustration. I had hardly begun to question him. I knew nothing else…at least, not a great deal. I wanted names, people I could contact, connections.

You didn't move fast enough, I chided myself.

He smiled at me, but his eyes remained dark. "You would be welcome to stop by any time to pick it up," he said. "It shouldn't take me more than two or three days to get it all together and ready for you. And of course… I will be more than happy to see you."

There he was, the coy cat I had met the first time… with everything but the swishing tail.

"Very well," I said, getting to my feet. "I look forward to it. Thank you, Mr. Steeles."

"Oh, and don't worry about the payment," he said with a wave of his hand. "Whenever your father is ready will be more than fine with me. Painting you has been enjoyment enough on its own."

Miles stepped up beside me, his expression cool. "I will make sure to deliver your payment from Mr. Shipman, sir."

"Excellent," Mr. Steeles said, and he gathered up his belongings more quickly than he had the last time.

He departed a short time later, and I lingered at the window, watching him go.

I didn't particularly like the idea of returning to his studio, but what choice did I have? Maybe I would finally be able to ask him the questions I had meant to here.

And maybe I will be ready with them this time, I thought. *I must not freeze up or doubt myself.*

13

"Is he gone?"

Joan strode into the room, glancing at the parlor window that overlooked the street, the same window I had just watched Mr. Steeles from, as he made his way down the sidewalk in the direction of his studio.

"Yes, he's gone," I said, turning to greet her.

"Good," she said, crossing her arms as she came to join me at the window. She frowned. "There's something repellent about him."

"I could not agree more..." I muttered.

"What did you learn?" she asked. "Anything?"

I had explained to her my true goal before the portrait session began.

"A small something," I said. "Apparently he and

Mrs. Milbourn were not as close as he made me believe."

She furrowed her brow. "He lied to you?"

"Not exactly," Miles said, having gone back to work on Father's bookshelf. He pulled down one of the tomes and rearranged it into a new home at the end of the shelf. "He just left some important information out of his initial explanation."

Joan looked curiously at me.

"Apparently Mrs. Milbourn owed Mr. Steeles a sum of money," I said. "He had painted a commissioned piece for her, and she didn't approve and so she didn't pay."

"It's not surprising he would be displeased about that," Joan said.

"No, it isn't," I said. "But he also made it sound as if her mind had begun to deteriorate recently. She started to lose things, forget things... Her nonpayment could be as simple as that."

"And I can't help but wonder if she truly asked him to make something up for her, or if he did it of his own volition and hoped to persuade her into buying it," Miles said. "We have only his word that she commissioned the work. He seems the conniving sort who might invent a scheme to embarrass people into paying for what they never requested."

I blinked at him. "I hadn't considered that."

"It would be a nasty thing to do, but we have no

evidence he did it," Joan reminded us. "It's mere speculation at this point, based on nothing but a gut feeling that there's something slimy about him. And didn't you say he claimed she was his mentor?"

"He told me today that he might have misled me about that," I said. "Now I don't know what to think. All I know is that he didn't give me the chance to ask any of the questions I wanted to ask."

"What sort of questions?" Miles asked, brow furrowing.

"I wanted to learn names of mutual friends of his and hers that I could go talk to, maybe some connections that could point me in the right direction – " I said, but Miles cut me off.

"You're more likely to get information out of *him* than anyone else, in my opinion. Maybe that *is* speculation, but it's warranted."

"What about Mrs. Leavens?" I asked. "She might have denied it, but being on the board like she was – "

"I thought you had dismissed her, given the way she reacted in her grief over her son's downturn? Her fight with the board had nothing to do with Mrs. Milbourn," Joan said.

I frowned. "Perhaps, but in her grief she still might have taken it out on Mrs. Milbourn. People do strange things when they're under a great deal of emotional pressure. Violent things, sometimes."

"Unlikely," Miles said. "Your original reasoning as

to why she was not a good suspect was sound. Don't second guess yourself now just to try and find answers that aren't there."

"Then Miss Turner – " I said. "Already a criminal, right? She might have – " But then I stopped again. I shook my head. "No...I don't feel like it was her. She didn't seem clever enough to have planned and gotten away with it."

"She might be a thief, but that doesn't automatically mean she's a killer," Miles agreed.

Joan scoffed. "How strange could this whole thing get?" she asked.

I stared between the two of them. "I don't have any other suspects. You think it could be Mr. Steeles?" I asked.

"He wanted money from her. That seems like a good enough reason," Joan said. "How long ago did that happen?"

"Almost three years ago," I said.

Her eyes widened. "And he's *still* upset about it? Even after her death?"

"You're right. I'm thinking about this entirely wrong," I said. "Why would he still be angry about it? If he really did admire her as much as he claimed to, he would have forgiven that in a heartbeat after finding out what happened to her, right? He likely never would have mentioned it, least of all to a stranger like me."

"That makes a great deal of sense," Miles said. "At the very least, it seems to be a good place to go from."

"When is he supposed to come back for another sitting?" Joan asked.

"He isn't," I said. "He's done. He asked me to go and pick up the portrait at his studio in a few days when he's finished framing it."

Joan snapped her fingers in frustration, turning away.

"I will just need to speak with him then," I said.

"Perhaps..." Miles said. "But what we really need is a means of finding more information. We need a plan."

"We?" I asked, looking back and forth at the pair of them.

"Well, yes," Joan said. "We have been helping you this whole time. What, did you think you were going to do this alone?"

"I have no idea what I am going to do," I said. "I'm not even entirely confident that Mr. Steeles did this."

"Nor am I," said Miles. "Then we might need to go early and find some information."

I glanced at him. "You will have to forgive me, but I don't wish to have a repeat of what happened that time we went after my uncle's killer."

To my surprise, he nodded. "I entirely agree," he said. "I made a grave mistake that night, allowing myself to be caught when I was. That was utter foolishness, and I apologize for what ensued because of my negligence. I can assure you it will *not* happen again."

I frowned ever so slightly. Was there any way he could guarantee that? If he was caught...but then again...

"It isn't as if I was any better," I admitted. "I froze up – " I shook my head. "That doesn't matter right now. What does matter is that we figure out a way to get some sort of information about Mr. Steeles without becoming suspect ourselves."

"He seems careful about his reputation," Miles said, folding his arms. "If anyone started sniffing around about him, he would be sure to find out."

"So then what can we do?" Joan asked.

I glanced out the window. The answer was plain to me, as I was sure it would have to be to Miles. The only trouble was that it would have to be something I did alone. "Joan, you must stay out of this, whatever we decide to do," I told her.

She glared at me. "Why?" she asked.

"You may not realize how dangerous it is, but – " I began.

"I don't care," she snapped, her eyes flashing. "This involves me too."

"It may have at the beginning," I said. "But if anything goes wrong – "

"Then it would be better for you not to be alone."

"Joan," I said, my voice rising to cover hers.

She stopped, blinking at me.

"You will stay here," I said. "Where it is safe."

We stood there for a few moments, staring at one another.

I could likely count on one hand the number of times I had enacted my authority as the older sister. Normally, I allowed Joan to take control. I *preferred* it even. But this time was different.

"I think Miss Sylvia is right," Miles said. "The more people involved in this, the greater the danger."

"But what of her?" Joan snapped. "She can go off and put herself in danger? That's foolishness to the highest degree."

"I have some experience in the matter – " I said.

"One time," Joan argued. "One time you went off and captured a killer. This is different. What if Steeles attacks you? I could be of help."

"Miss Joan, Miss Sylvia is right that you should not be – " Miles said.

Joan didn't let him finish, but made a frustrated sound, whirled around, and stalked from the room.

"You did the right thing," Miles said, beside me. "At least now she will be safe."

"Yes, I know," I said. "I need some time to think now. I will be in my room."

I strode out of the room and up the stairs, knowing that Joan had likely locked herself in her bedroom. When I reached my own room, I slipped in and closed the door. The quiet shadows enveloped me, and I let out a sigh that quickly was absorbed by the stillness.

I had already come up with a plan. My mind had been formulating one even as I spoke with Joan and Miles. I knew what I needed to do.

And regardless of what Miles thought...I knew I had to go and do it alone.

14

The last time I had been so nervous while taking a taxi was when I was just sixteen. Mother and Father had forgotten me at a charity ball, and while I had waited around for them for almost two hours, it had become quite clear that they had either not noticed, or had no intention of coming to retrieve me. I had to have Father go out to the cabby to pay him when I finally returned home, and received little more than a qualified apology for leaving me behind.

Today, though, would certainly take first place.

I thanked the driver, giving him a hefty tip. He pocketed it, looking up at me as I stood shivering on the sidewalk. "You sure you don't want me to stick around for you? I'd hate to leave you out in the freezing cold like this."

"Thank you," I said. "But I have no idea how long I might be here. It would be better for me to simply call another driver."

He shrugged then, and drove off.

I had asked him to drop me off across the street from Mr. Steeles' studio building. A familiar melody tickled my ears from a piano in one of the nearby buildings, though I wondered how anyone could leave their window open in these frigid temperatures. I caught the scent of something roasted, with garlic and onion, and my mouth watered.

Night had just begun to fall, the last of the pink in the sky bleeding into violet, then inky black overhead. A buzz like an enormous insect sounded over my head, and I looked up just in time to see one of the street lamps flicker to life.

I shivered again, drawing my coat more tightly around my shoulders as I kept my lonely vigil, staring at the windows of what I knew to be Mr. Steeles' studio across the street. I waited and waited, keeping a close eye...until suddenly, the lights within went off, and the windows became dark.

Just what I wanted to see, I thought, but did not yet move. Though tremors of cold wracked my body, the tense muscles in my back aching from the bite of the wind, I waited. I wanted to be perfectly sure that he was truly gone.

After another ten minutes of sitting there, without

any movement in the windows, I thought it likely safe to go. I glanced down the street for any oncoming traffic before I stepped onto the pavers.

I wasn't terribly surprised to find the door into the building proper was unlocked. When Miles and I had been here the last time, it had been the same way. I quickly shook the memory from my mind. Best not to think of Miles or what he would say when he realized I had come here all on my own. I had no choice. It would be far easier to catch two people sneaking around than one. On my own, I could be invisible.

I did my best to look as if I was supposed to be there, keeping my head high and my expression neutral. I didn't pass anyone on the stairs as I made my way up to Mr. Steeles' studio, but my heart thundered so hard inside my chest that I had to hold the railing so as not to sway too much. When I finally reached the landing, I stretched my hand out and tried the door –

Locked.

My hopes sank. I shouldn't have expected it to be open, but I *needed* it to be.

I stared at the door, willing it to open right there before my very eyes.

It did not.

I lingered there, wondering what I should do. I had come all this way for...what? Nothing.

I really should have thought this through a little more, I reprimanded myself. *I should have come up with some idea of what to do if I couldn't get in –*

"Are you looking for Julian?"

My heart nearly burst out of my chest as I wheeled around.

A man in his mid to late forties stood at the bottom of the stairwell behind me. He reached up to push the bridge of his glasses up his narrow nose.

I noted the smock he wore, flecked with paint. *Another artist,* I thought.

"Oh – " I said nervously. "Y – Yes, I am." I needed to think quickly. What if he told Mr. Steeles that I was trying to break in?

The man took the stairs slowly, but with a graceful familiarity. *He must work here,* I thought. "A patron of his?" he asked.

"Yes, I am," I said. *He must be used to seeing people coming in and out for Mr. Steeles, then. That is good news for me,* I thought with a modicum of relief.

He smirked as he reached the top of the steps. "Ah, yes, a *patron*," he said. This close, I noticed the green in his eyes that reminded me briefly of Miles. He withdrew a ring of keys, beginning to flick through them like a deck of cards. He chuckled as he selected a key, slid it into the lock of Mr. Steeles' door, and pushed the door open. He stood aside to let me pass.

I could only stare at him. *Could it truly be this easy?* I thought.

His smile widened. "Don't look so dumbfounded," he said with a chuckle. "I hold spare keys to all the apartments and studios, in case of emergency." Then his face softened. "Oh dear…not another one."

"Another one?" I asked.

He sighed, shaking his head. "You don't know, do you?" he asked. "What am I saying? Of course you don't. You wouldn't be so surprised if you did."

"About what?" I asked.

He pursed his lips, then gave me another pitying look. "Listen…I really wish I didn't have to be the one to tell you this…the one to tell several of you…but Julian often has multiple…*patrons* in his life at a time. And most of them don't know about the others. I'm sorry to be the bearer of bad news. Maybe it would be best if you got your things and left him behind. You're a pretty girl. Surely there is someone else you could choose."

I nodded. "Thank you…" I said, allowing him to believe my shock at my good fortune was the distress of a broken heart.

I got what I wanted, didn't I? I thought. *I didn't have to pick any locks or crawl through any windows…*

"Take your time," the man said. "I'm sure he won't be back until morning."

I walked past him into the studio, looking around as the man started back down the stairs.

I closed the door behind me, and let out a breath I hadn't realized I had been keeping.

*All right, Miles...*I thought. *If you were here...where would you start looking?*

I started in, passing by tables laden with blank canvases, boxes filled with paintbrushes, and tubes of paint spotted with dried blotches of entirely different colors than the strip beneath the cap.

My insides twisted around themselves, and I stared around in dismay. Where *would* I find anything? How could I possibly dig through this mess and hope to stumble upon anything?

Think, Sylvia, think! I told myself. If I worked here, where would I put something about my mentor?

What if he wouldn't have kept anything here? I suddenly thought with dismay. *What if he brought anything that might tie him to Mrs. Milbourn back to his own residence?*

If that was the case...then I had no hope of finding anything here, and this was nothing more than a giant waste of time.

Nevertheless, I had to try.

I crossed to the back of the room, to the cabinet that he had been looking in the first time I had come here. In the dark, it was difficult to navigate around the table legs and the easels. I nearly tripped over one of them, only managing with a loud gasp to catch myself on the back of a wooden chair.

Heart pounding, I allowed myself a moment to catch my breath. *That could have been horrendous...* There would be no hiding that I had been here, if I stumbled into one of his paintings and damaged it.

I reached the cabinet, drawing the doors open. There did seem to be personal affects within, including a number of coats all lazily folded on one shelf. I found a few notebooks filled with sketches, and a satchel that contained...nothing.

I sighed.

A glint caught my eye as I moved to close the cabinet door, and squinting into the darkness of the shelves, I drew in a sharp breath.

A perfect glass sphere sat upon the shelf, atop a velvety green pillow. It looked as if it were made of ice, smooth and perfect like a soap bubble.

That orb...it's just like the one at the exhibit! I thought.

Gingerly, I reached inside to draw it out.

It was the very same shape as the one Mrs. Milbourn had been admiring the night of the attack. We had spoken about it.

Questions flashed through my mind; was this her creation? Was it Mr. Steeles'? Had she seen it that night, wanting to admire his work? Why had he hidden it away like this?

I turned it over in my hands, more certain with every passing second that it was exactly like the one we had seen at the gallery, if not *the* orb that –

"What are you doing here?"

I gasped...and the orb slipped out of my hands, shattering as it struck the travertine marble floor below.

15

"Miss Shipman? Is that you?"

The silhouette of Mr. Steeles stood in the doorframe, haloed in the light that spilled over the threshold from the hall behind him.

"I – " I started, nausea sloshing my stomach. I could only gape down at the splintered pieces of glass. "I'm so sorry, I didn't mean to – "

As quickly as that, he was standing right in front of me, as lithe as the cat his grins seemed to reflect. I could barely make out the shape of his face as he looked down at the orb. "It's perfectly all right," he surprised me by saying, using the inside of his shoe to sweep away the shards that tinkled as they obediently slipped out of sight. "I have about a dozen more of them."

That answers that question, I suppose, I thought somewhere in the clearer parts of my mind.

"I'm so very sorry," I said. "I saw it and I – "

"They're quite lovely, aren't they?" he asked. He took another step toward me. "I would be happy to give you another, if that's what you were hoping for. But first...I do wonder about the reason for this unexpected visit? Imagine my surprise when I came back to my studio to fetch a forgotten sketch book...only to find you here."

I swallowed hard, uncertain what to say. Sweat beaded along my hairline, as my mind raced to find any possible explanation I could give for snooping around his studio in the dark. Did he already know? Did he suspect what had brought me here?

His hand reached up over his head, and he tugged on a thin cord. Instantly, light blasted down from a bulb above.

"I am just here for my painting," I finally said, fumbling for an excuse, however weak.

His smile faltered and he tilted his head to the side slightly. "But I only just saw you this afternoon," he said. Then he laughed. "Oh, *I* see..." he said, his expression changing. "You knew full well that it wouldn't be done, but simply wanted a reason to see me again. It's all perfectly clear now."

Was it, though?

"I think the truth..." he said, leaning toward me, "... is that you wanted more of my attention. Is that right?"

I hesitated, resisting the impulse to take a step backward. Out of all the excuses I might give, that one hadn't occurred to me.

"Oh, come now, Miss Shipman..." he said. "I've seen the way you look at me, casting longing glances my way when I have been painting your portrait. I know you've been thinking the same thing I have...haven't you?"

My heart thundered as he moved closer, making me feel trapped. I blurted out the only thing I could think of.

"Did you kill Mrs. Milbourn?"

The question tumbled from my lips before I had even thought through it properly.

The look in his eyes was immediately replaced by an icy chill. He glared down at me, disturbing shadows swaying beneath his eyes from the ever so slightly swinging light over our heads. "What did you say?" he breathed.

"I want to know if you are the one who murdered Mrs. Milbourn." My voice sounded braver than I felt.

"I have no idea what you're talking about..." he growled.

He does, a voice at the back of my mind whispered. *He knows exactly what you're talking about.*

He turned and started away from me, and for a

wild moment, I thought he was going to leave the studio all together.

He didn't, however; instead, he snatched a ceramic vessel curing on a table and smashed it against the floor.

The ear-shattering sound sent shivers down my spine, and I clapped my hands over my ears even as I ducked down behind the nearest table in a pool of shadow.

"What do you know, hmm?" Mr. Steeles barked, his pacing footsteps echoing off the room. "If you're here saying such things – you must know something! Now tell me, what is it?"

My heart pounded fiercely in my chest.

"Who was it that told you?" he hissed, kicking a chair as he passed by it. "Was it Philip? Or Sherman? Or perhaps Mrs. Leavens?"

Mrs. Leavens? What would she know? I wondered. I had no idea who the other people he spoke of were. Perhaps fellow artists who had suspicions about him?

"Someone had to have put those thoughts into your head," he said. "Someone had to have made you afraid of me, to make you think I could do something so violent..."

I stayed behind the table, peering through its legs at him as he made long strides through the middle of the studio. The table didn't conceal me much, but at least it would offer some sort of shield if he were to hurl anything in my direction.

"No one in this town can keep a secret!" he spat, and he stopped in his tracks. "They just cannot keep their mouths *shut*!"

Was he even talking to me any longer? Did he even care that I was hearing what he was spouting off?

"No one understands," he muttered, resuming his nervous pacing. "No one would ever understand, would they? They didn't know what she was like, how she...*chided* me. She never wanted me to succeed. All she ever wanted was *perfection.*"

I slowly lifted my eyes over the table. He had his hands pressed to either side of his temples, massaging his skull.

"Didn't she know I could never be like her?" he hissed through his clenched teeth. "Why wouldn't she understand that I had my *own* methods, my own ideas! But then she would just stare at me with that – that *look* that demeaned me, belittled me, even while she *lied* to my face!" His voice rose to a shout, as he swept his hand over a nearby table, sweeping papers and pencils off onto the floor.

I glanced at the door, where a brilliant shaft of light glowed, no more than a sliver. It was too far away. I would never reach it in time.

How was I going to get out of here?

I had to buy myself some time.

"No one knows," I said, my voice cracking from behind the table.

His nervous pacing ceased for a moment. "What do you mean?"

I said, "I don't know if anyone else knows." It was a foolish thing to admit, but I was desperate to keep him talking. Every moment we spent talking gave him a little more time to calm down.

"You don't know if there's anyone else?" Mr. Steeles asked.

I stood up, finally facing him.

"If you know, if *you* know, then surely there are others who do," he said. "And *what* do you know? I've admitted to nothing."

He stopped, his eyes widening.

"If you..." he breathed, his eyes sweeping sightlessly around the floor. "If *you* know...then what hope do I have?"

He stood there for a long time, as still as the many portraits smiling hollowly out at me.

This wasn't good.

I glanced back toward the door, my pulse racing.

"I have to...do something..." he mumbled.

Slowly, he reached down for the shards of the orb. His fingers swept through the glittering dust until he selected one of the biggest pieces. He slowly lifted it, his eyes turning toward me. He dragged the tip along the floor, and goosebumps flared up on my arms and neck as it screeched across the tiles.

The broken shard was obviously sharp enough to make a good weapon.

I had no choice. It was either try to reach the door and possibly fail, or stand here in shock and certainly die.

Suddenly, as I prepared to move, light burst from the doorway. A shadowed figure shot into the room, heading straight for Mr. Steeles.

The two figures collided and fell to the floor in a clamor of shouts and grunts.

I gasped, hurrying around the table just in time to see Miles pinning Mr. Steeles' to the floor, both his arms drawn tightly behind his back.

"Get off me!" Mr. Steeles bellowed.

"I don't think I will," Miles said through gritted teeth.

"Miles, what are you – " I cried.

I jumped out of the way as Miles' arm reached past me. "Grab something to tie him with! Hurry!" he cried.

"Uh – right," I said, turning this way and that. I spotted a spool of twine and hurried to retrieve it. I found a pair of scissors as I made my way back to him.

I cut off a few feet of twine, while Mr. Steeles continued to struggle on the floor. It looked as if at any moment he would wriggle into a position where he could flip Miles off him.

Following Miles' instructions, I wrapped the twine several times around Mr. Steeles' wrists. "There we are," Miles said as I drew the string so tight Mr. Steeles let out a cry of pain, the string digging into his flesh. "Up we go, now."

Miles hoisted the artist upright, and then slammed him down into a nearby chair.

Using more twine, he tied the knotted loops around Mr. Steeles' wrists to the frame of the chair and secured his legs to the chair, as well.

"There..." Miles said, swiping the back of his hand over his now glistening brow. "Time to pay the piper, Steeles. I see no reason for you to attack Miss Sylvia unless you were the one to kill Mrs. Milbourn. Don't waste your breath trying to convince me otherwise."

Mr. Steeles spat on the floor near Miles' feet. "You're not the police," he said. "I don't have to tell you anything."

I crossed my arms, my heart still beating uncomfortably in my chest. "You might as well admit to it," I said. "The way you went on about how little she appreciated you, how she chided you – "

"She thought I was a fool for trying new artistic methods and mediums. That I lacked the talent," Mr. Steeles said, his eyes bulging as he strained against his bindings. "All she ever had for me was contempt!"

"And so you killed her?" Miles asked.

Mr. Steeles lashed out, the chair screeching across

the tiles a few inches. "I couldn't take it anymore! The lies, the sneers... She thought I was – "

"You are all wrong about her," I interrupted.

Both men shifted their gazes back to me.

"I saw her the night of the gallery opening," I said. "She gazed at one of those orbs you made with such affection, such admiration. I didn't know it at the time, but I see now that she was proud of it. By extension... proud of you."

Mr. Steeles' nasty look morphed into one of horror. "She...what?"

I shook my head, waving a hand. "You don't deserve to hear it," I said. "Just know you were wrong. You can live with that every day for the rest of your life."

Miles moved quickly then, ushering me out into the hall before Mr. Steeles could say anything else.

"Would you go downstairs, find one of the neighbors, and have them telephone the police?" he asked.

"All right," I said. "Meanwhile, what about Steeles?"

"I'll stay with him. I won't let him out of my sight until he is in police custody," he said. "With any luck, he'll confess to them."

"Right..." I said, my relief palpable now that it was all over. "How did you know I was here?" I asked as Miles turned to go back into the studio.

He smiled. "I think I have come to know you well enough to understand how your mind works," he said.

"After our conversation about all this, I knew you would be determined to come here. What I hadn't considered at first was that you would come on your own. That was a big risk to take."

My cheeks colored, but I didn't apologize. "It was necessary," I pointed out. "He would never have confessed so much if you or anyone else had been here with me."

"Perhaps not," he said. "But may I be so bold as to suggest you not endanger yourself this way again?"

"I will do my best," I said.

But as he walked away, I admitted to myself it was a promise I might not be able to keep...

16

"I do feel a little guilty," I said, watching the flames in the fireplace eat up the canvas that had been delivered just a short time before. "Father spent money on this, after all."

"Did he, though?" Joan asked with a shrug. "I don't think he had even managed to get the money to Mr. Steeles yet. I'm not sure how he could, since that awful man now sits in a prison cell, awaiting trial. I hear he confessed all to the police."

I shivered, thinking about Mrs. Milbourn and how a single unfortunate encounter had cost her life.

The amber flames licked up the painting, the oil melting into streaks like red and black droplets of rain. My stomach clenched as I stared into Mr. Steeles' version of my own eyes, watching as the image faded into ashes.

"It really wasn't very good," Joan said, shaking her head. "He didn't capture you well enough, if you ask me. Mediocre, at best."

She looked sidelong at me. "I saw you writing a letter this afternoon," she said, off handedly.

"I was," I said. "To Mr. Adams."

"Oh?" she asked, brows lifting. "And?"

"I thanked him for all the fun we'd had together, but explained I am going to be busy for the foreseeable future with some new opportunities," I said.

"So you didn't exactly say no to him, did you?" Joan asked.

"I think he will know what I meant," I said. "He's a smart man."

She shrugged. "Perhaps you should have just told him you're in love with someone else."

"Don't be ridiculous," I scoffed. "There is no one else."

She regarded me with amusement. "I was suggesting it as a polite fib, to discourage him from pursuing you further," she said. "But as I've said before, it's obvious to everyone but you that someone has, in fact, attracted your interest. No, you don't have to tell me who. I'll figure it out for myself. I think I might even figure it out before *you* do."

With that, she turned with a laugh and made her way from the room.

I stood there next to the fire until the entire canvas

had been consumed, and found that once it was gone, I felt a great deal better. It was as if I could put Mr. Steeles in the past and keep him there, without any physical evidence that he had ever been a part of my life.

That, and it had been more than gratifying to toss it into the hearth in the first place.

Miles will be happy to know we are rid of it, I thought. *Maybe I should inform him before I turn in for the night.*

I headed out into the hall, listening for his signature whistling. I assumed he might be upstairs, perhaps tidying up my father's study, or maybe down in the kitchen –

I caught a glimpse of him at the end of the hall, passing by through the foyer. I started that way.

I opened my mouth to draw his attention as I reached the end of the hall. But before I could speak, I saw him slip through the back door, out onto the veranda and into the back garden.

Odd, I thought, following after him. *What's he doing out there at this time of night?*

I pushed the door open, stepping out into the frigid night air. As soon as I started across the veranda, I regretted not grabbing my coat – or anyone's coat, really – from the coat closet.

Miles hadn't noticed me, but he kept looking right and left, even at this hour when there would be no one out and about to disturb him.

Where is he going? I thought, watching as he continued on toward the edge of the river all the way at the far side of the property.

My nerves began to hum and the tiny hairs at the back of my neck stood up.

Something wasn't right.

All at once, my suspicions came flooding back, even after I had chosen to set those worries about him aside.

*He doesn't want to be seen...*I thought.

I started across the lawn until I realized I was leaving footprints in the frosted grass, and so, hurried to one of the low walls along the path instead. I followed the wall, until it began to curve.

My heart starting to race, I glanced around the corner of the wall up ahead.

Miles approached the edge of the river, looking back and forth a few more times before reaching into the front of his jacket.

He withdrew a small item wrapped in cloth. For a moment, he simply held it clutched in his hand. Then he drew his arm back and tossed the bundle hard into the river.

He stood there for a few moments, watching the rippling water until the currents smoothed out and resumed their trajectory.

What in the world was that? I wondered. Whatever it

was, it was clear he never had any intention of retrieving it.

What could he have been so desperate to destroy?

At once, I thought back to that newspaper article I had found…and the photo of him standing beside that woman…a woman now dead.

He hurried back to the house, passing right by the spot where I was hiding without noticing me.

After he was gone, I lingered there in the cold, trying to make sense of what I had seen. My mind was scrambling to concoct a reasonable explanation for his action, but I forced it to stop. I had to look at this rationally.

Why had I continually found myself relying on a man who behaved in such strange, suspicious ways? Did it matter how many risks and dangers we had already faced together? Did it matter that he was quickly proving indispensable to my family? Did it matter that I wanted to trust him more than anything?

Maybe it didn't, maybe none of it mattered.

Because if Miles wasn't who he said he was…if Miles did in fact kill his wife back in London…

Maybe his past wasn't his own business after all. Maybe it was time I finally got to the bottom of it.

Continue the mysterious adventures of Sylvia Shipman in "Murder With Method: A Sylvia Shipman Murder Mystery Book 3."

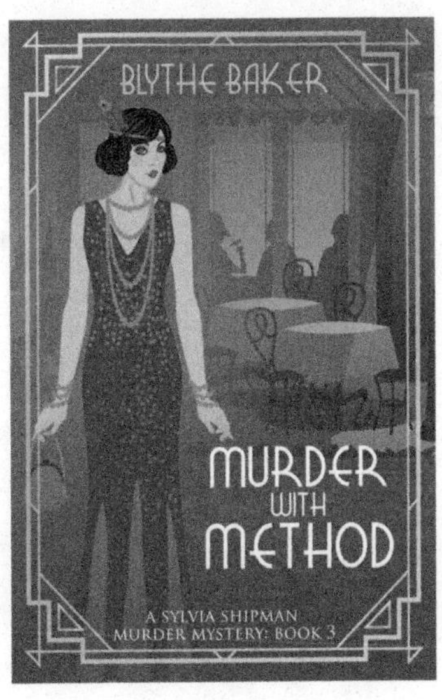

ABOUT THE AUTHOR

Blythe Baker is the lead writer behind several popular historical and paranormal mystery series. When Blythe isn't buried under clues, suspects, and motives, she's acting as chauffeur to her children and head groomer to her household of beloved pets. She enjoys walking her dogs, lounging in her backyard hammock, and fiddling with graphic design. She also likes binge-watching mystery shows on TV. To learn more about Blythe, visit her website and sign up for her newsletter at www.blythebaker.com